英韵经典唐诗百首

Classic Tang Poems in English Rhyme

霍红　译

中国海洋大学出版社
·青岛·

图书在版编目(CIP)数据

英韵经典唐诗百首 / 霍红译 . -- 青岛：中国海洋大学出版社，2024. 5

ISBN 978-7-5670-3851-6

Ⅰ. ①英… Ⅱ. ①霍… Ⅲ. ①唐诗－英语－翻译－研究 Ⅳ. ①I207. 22 ②H315. 9

中国国家版本馆 CIP 数据核字(2024)第 097152 号

出版发行	中国海洋大学出版社		
社　　址	青岛市香港东路 23 号	邮政编码	266071
出 版 人	刘文菁		
网　　址	http://pub.ouc.edu.cn		
订购电话	0532－82032573(传真)		
责任编辑	邵成军	电　　话	0532－85902533
印　　制	青岛国彩印刷股份有限公司		
版　　次	2024 年 5 月第 1 版		
印　　次	2024 年 5 月第 1 次印刷		
成品尺寸	170 mm ×230 mm		
印　　张	15. 5		
字　　数	60 千		
印　　数	1—1 000		
定　　价	125. 00 元		

译者简介

霍红

2001年成都理工大学英语专业毕业，获文学学士学位；2006年澳大利亚莫纳什大学国际英语教学专业毕业，获教育学硕士学位；2013年至2014年在美国俄克拉何马州立大学英语系访学；2015年上海外国语大学英语语言文学专业毕业，获博士学位；2015年至2021年，于扬州大学文学院做博士后。现为扬州大学外国语学院副教授，硕士生导师。主要学术兴趣包括文学翻译、语用学及二语习得。系江苏省翻译工作者协会会员。主持江苏省教育厅哲学社会科学研究项目1项，主持校级科研项目多项，出版教材2部，出版《海棠依旧·霍红双语诗集选》自创自译中英双语格律诗著作1部，多篇翻译作品在《英语世界》等期刊发表。

The Translator's Profile

Huo Hong, who received a Bachelor's degree in English literature from Chengdu University of Technology in 2001, a Master's degree in TESOL from Monash University, Australia in the December of 2005, a doctoral degree in English language and literature from Shanghai International Studies University in 2015 and who was a visiting scholar to the English department of Oklahoma State University, the US from the December of 2013 to that of 2014 and was doing postdoctoral research at College of Humanities of Yangzhou University from December, 2015 to June, 2021, is now an associate professor of College of International Studies of Yangzhou University, who supervises postgraduates and whose academic interest covers literary translation, pragmatics and so on. As a member of Jiangsu Translators Association, she is found productive in books and research papers, has undertaken one provincial project funded by Educational Department of Jiangsu Province and was involved in compiling two textbooks. Keen on translating traditional Chinese poems though, she has translated some literary works such as English-translated essays published in *The English World*. More than what relates her career, she is a poet who has had a poem selection of her own published, namely *Gone and Go On* in both Chinese and English.

序

悠悠五千年，泱泱大中华。中华民族五千多年的辉煌文明是世界的瑰宝，是国人的骄傲，它成为凝聚中华民族的精神力量，是中华民族文化自信的支撑和动力。

在中国经济历经了几十年的蓬勃发展之后，中国的航天、航空以及通信等科技已走在了世界前列，中国在各个领域的不断发展强大提升了国学的热度，这是中国以自身的发展而创造的历史。这个时期是令中国人民走出历经近代史的沧桑和满是疮痍的旧中国、走进独立自主的辉煌新时代中国历史的重要转折期，是中华儿女为祖国所拥有的一切而自豪的时代。国学热，是历史缔造的呼唤，是中国新时代形象塑造的途径，是中华民族伟大复兴的诉求。物质的不断富足，更需要精神上的丰满和自信。在中华民族复兴的征途上，经济、科技及人才的丰稔，为精神的高昂奠定了强大的物质基础，而我们中华民族赖以维系的、赖以团结的精神力量恰恰来自浩瀚的中国历史和博大的中华文化。因此，我们必须培养传承及发扬中国传统文化的意识。

“要挖掘中华优秀传统文化的思想观念、人文精神、道德规范，把艺术创造力和中华文化价值融合起来，把中华美学精神和当代审美追求结合起来，激活中华文化生命力。故步自封、陈陈相因谈不上传承，割断血脉、凭空虚造不能算创新。要把握传承和创新的关系，学古不泥古、破法不悖法，让中华优秀传统文化成为文艺创新的重要源泉。”

——2021 年 12 月 14 日，习近平在中国文联十一大、中国作协十大开幕式上的讲话

“中华文明延续着我们国家和民族的精神血脉，既需要薪火相传、代代守护，也需要与时俱进、推陈出新。要加强对中华优秀传统文化的挖掘和阐发，使中华民族最基本的文化基因与当代文化相适应、与现代社会相协调，把跨越时空、超越国界、富有永恒魅力、具有当代价值的文化精神弘扬起来。”

——2016 年 5 月 17 日，习近平在哲学社会科学工作座谈会上的讲话

国学就是中国的传统文化，是中国几千年以来形成的优秀的文化内容，且国学往往是中国固有的文化中最核心的、最具有文化特征的、最能体现中华民族智慧的内容。国学的精髓恰恰存在于经典之中。对于传统文化的继承，须对经典了解并具有新时代下的重新诠释，在继承中更新认识，在继承中重新发现，所以是传承，也是发扬，是古为今用，是文化的接力与不断缔造。改革开放四十多年以来，虽经历了西方文化的强势涌入，然而在了解了更多西方文化后的中国，我们以更开放的心境来认识并了解西方文化后，更加能够具有自我文化意识并摆正中华民族自身所具有的文化及文化精神在我们心中的位置——保持自我，才能屹立民族之林。

经典，通常指那些具有典范性的、权威性的，具有民族文化特征的著作或文献。唐诗，是经典中的经典，它是汉文字音意相协、言简意深的最高水平的呈现。朗朗上口、脍炙人口的诗篇，令人或领略到唐朝的盛况、繁华及辉煌，或感受到盛世后的衰落、萧条及黯然，诗人的潇洒恣意、沉郁顿挫、忧国忧民、恬淡自洽等情愫，均化在诗歌的字里行间，令人遐思，令人动容。唐朝的诗歌，凝聚了唐朝诗人的人生与生命智慧，是唐朝历史的解锁之匙，是我们探索唐人心绪的时空穿梭机，是文学之林中一朵永不败落的奇葩，是中华

民族引以为豪的文学和历史现象。

屹立于世界民族之林，不仅依赖经济、科技以及人才，更有赖于优秀的民族文化。英国的文学、德国的哲学、波兰的音乐等在精神领域上于世界的传播，令其源国以文化闻名于世界，且比起他们国家的其他物质文明，这些文化好似刻入民族基因里的存在而更令世界瞩目和惊叹。我们的国家具有更悠久的历史和文化，中国的传统哲学、诗歌等不应仅仅属于中国，而应让世界知晓。国学的翻译是让世界了解国学的途径，是在世界范围传播中华文化，是向世界展现国学经典的文辞之美和哲学思想。

唐朝文学形式中最光彩夺目的、成就最高的莫属唐诗。唐诗，泛指唐朝诗人所作的诗歌，包括五言、六言、七言、五绝、六绝、七绝、五律、六律、七律以及词，在音韵表意的结合方面可谓登峰造极，是唐朝文人的智慧结晶。唐诗开始对格律等要求更加严格，逐渐形成了人们熟知的“近体诗”，对字数、句数、平仄、押韵等进行了更为苛刻的限定，具有独特的艺术魅力和文化价值。近体诗的创作难度大，对诗人的艺术修养和文学素养要求高。

自从晚清国门打开，中国与世界有了不断联系之后，便不断有外国译者和中国译者从事国学经典的翻译，从《诗经》到唐诗、到宋词。然而，他们多数采用散译、释译的翻译方式，尽管大多译诗还原了原诗的文辞之美，却未能做到“以诗译诗”，或者说未能以“译诗”呈现原诗的神韵，比如中国古诗中的韵、音节数量等的限定并未在译诗中得以体现。直到许渊冲的译诗出现，方才打破了一直以来的散译模式，这是中国传统诗歌翻译的创举，开启了中国古诗词格律音韵翻译的时代。使唐诗的译文具有与唐诗无限接近的含蕴与形式，是翻译，亦是绞尽脑汁的创作，对译者的文字功底和文学修养有极高的要求。

“音韵译诗，以诗译诗”是许渊冲翻译的重要形式和翻译诗学观。双语在细节上的相似是源语艺术性传递到译文中的一种努力，这不仅仅是将源语中的“音美”与“形美”代入进了译文，也是将中华文学艺术特征代入进了译文。许渊冲提出的“三美”翻译诗学观主要包括"意美""音美"与"形美",以此令诗魂也借生于译诗当中。然而,唐诗中的诸多元素,诸如对仗等修辞、意象以及中国艺术作品中常用的留白手法,有的在译诗中未得到还原,因而使译诗在某种程度上失去了原诗的深远意境和艺术魅力。

"如果同一文本存在两个或更多的相同译入语译文,新译文往往比早期出现的译文更加接近原文。"(Paloposki & Koskinen, 2004)对国学经典翻译的精益求精是后来翻译者的向往与追求,翻译者孜孜不倦地对译诗进行无限接近原诗的探索是国学经典对外传播的动力。赵彦春教授的《英韵唐诗百首》(*Tang Poems in English Rhyme*)正体现了译者探寻更佳译诗的精神和努力。本书作者同样秉承着这样的精神,也做着与前辈们相似的努力。

令读英译唐诗有读唐诗的感觉,这是从许渊冲教授到赵彦春教授、再到我等后辈翻译者的执着,是对如晖如曦的中华文化之挚爱的抒发。中华文化博大精深,唐朝诗歌隽永绚烂,如一首令人陶醉的歌,应累世诵吟,举世传唱。

霍 红

2024 年 2 月于扬州

Preface

Magnificent is China, with a history of more than five thousand years. The splendid Chinese culture is the treasure of the world, the pride of the Chinese people, the spiritual strength for the cohesion of the Chinese nation, and the prop and power for the nation's cultural confidence.

After decades of rapid development in economy, China has ranked top in aviation, aeronautics and tele-communication in recent years. China's continuing advances on all fronts has led to more kindled fervour for Chinese ancient civilization studies, bringing in a history made through China's painstaking struggles forward, a turning point in history where the Chinese people hauled themselves out of misery and the old China in trauma, forging ahead into an independence-maintaining and self-strengthening era, and an epoch in which the Chinese people take pride in what their country holds in possession. Ardour for Chinese ancient civilization studies is called for as a history reshaper, an approach to a whole new China reshaping, a resort to rejuvenating the Chinese nation. As material wealth grows ample, spiritual richness and confidence are required to be well-matched. On the journey to the national rejuvenation, it is the spiritual strength that brings the Chinese people together despite that the plentitude in economy, technology and talent has prepared China on the material basis for holding our heads high. The awareness of passing down and carrying forward traditional Chinese culture, therefore, ought to be fostered.

"Dig for excellent thoughts and concepts, humanistic spirit and moral

norm out of traditional Chinese culture, merge creativity of art and the value of Chinese culture, and integrate Chinese aesthetic spirit and modern aesthetics to endow Chinese culture with vitality. Complacency, conservativeness and pursuit of a set rule are far from tradition while the severing of the nation's cultural vein or fabrication out of nothing does not count as innovation. It is important that the relationship between historical inheritance and innovation be grasped, the old be learned rather than being rigidly adhered to, and the rule be broken rather than being unwisely violated to place excellent traditional Chinese culture in the role of the source of innovation in literature and art."

—Speech by Xi Jinping on Dec. 14, 2021 at the opening ceremony of the 11th National Congress of China Federation of Literary and Art Circles and the 10th National Congress of China Writers Association

"Not only does the Chinese civilization, a continued spiritual vein of our country and nation, require passing down from generation to generation and guardianship of all generations, but it also has to keep pace with the times and bring forth the new through the old. It is necessary to enhance the exploration and elucidation of excellent traditional Chinese culture, adapt the primary Chinese cultural genes to the modern culture, bring them in line with modern society, and carry forward the cultural spirit that passes through time and space and transcends national borders, equipped with eternal charm and loaded with modern cultural value."

—Speech by Xi Jinping at the symposium on philosophy and social science work

Referring largely to the traditional Chinese culture, the Chinese ancient civilization studies, which involves superb cultural elements that started off several thousand years ago, chances to be the core, culturally-featured, wisdom-embodying part of the inherited culture. The essence of the studies exists precisely in literary classics. To inherit the traditional Chinese culture, classics are supposed to be followed through a newly-interpreted version of exploration, knowledge updated in the process of being taken in, perception renewed in the process of being accepted and adopted, in which sense passing it down is conducted through carrying it forward, means that the ancient civilization is intended for the present, and is the relaying and continued reshaping of culture. Since the Opening-up and Reform launched over forty years ago, China that went through the Western culture's being dominant, with more exposure to it, has become more open to it. This has led China to the heightened awareness of its cultural confidence and the justified placement of the Chinese culture and the cultural spirit in the mind—Stick to our cultural features and the Chinese nation will be able to sustain itself in the world.

The classics, which are usually considered exemplary, authoritative and of high quality, tend to be embodied in culture-loaded literary books or literature on a particular subject. Concise in using Chinese characters with the uttermost sophistication, Tang poems reached the height of Chinese classics, marrying prosody with meaning. Agreeably catchy and widely-loved, they transport us either to the pomp, prosperity and glory of the Tang Dynasty or to the downward, sluggish and depressed state of it. The poets' soul freedom, unconstraint, gloom, misgivings about his country and people, indifference to fame and gain and their easy lives present themselves in between the lines, thought-provoking and captivating. Tang poets' lives and life wisdom drawn on, Tang poems, whose poetic art shines in the literary world, cast themselves in the role of unlocking the history of the Tang Dynasty and of a time machine that carries us back through history to explore the Tang people's minds.

To take an assured place among the world nations, excellent culture is in demand other than advanced economy, high technology and great talents. The spread of English literature of Shakespearean time, philosophy of Germany and music of Poland has brought their home culture to high world fame, which has won more focused, admirable attention of the world than the material civilization of their home countries. China, a country of a long history and culture, is the bed for philosophy, poetry and so on, all of which should not spread within a restricted range but beyond to the world. The translating of the Chinese ancient classic works offers an approach to letting them known to the world, with Chinese culture introduced, the beauty of language presented and philosophical thoughts open to the world.

Tang poetry is the crowning glory and the highest achievement of Tang literature. Tang poems, referring in a general sense to poems composed by poets of the Tang Dynasty, include five-character quatrains, six-character quatrains, seven-character quatrains, five-character metrical quatrains, six-character metrical quatrains, seven-character metrical quatrains, five-character metrical octaves, six-character metrical octaves, seven-character metrical octaves and lyrics, all of which, a representation of the Tang literati's wisdom, came to the peak of constructing meaning with sounds and rhythms. More requirements or composing rules added, gradually transformed into "modern style poems" that have rigid demanding restrictions on number of Chinese characters, number of sentences, level and oblique tone, and rhyme, Tang Poems have unique artistic charm and cultural value. The difficulty in composing modern style poems overwhelms that in composing poems of other styles, with poets' high artistic culture and literature attainment called for.

Since the door of the Late Qing Dynasty was forced open, which compelled China into the world flow, more and more translators from home and abroad have engaged in translating the Chinese classics from *Book of Poetry* to Tang poems and Song lyrics. However, their translated works come largely in the prose or explanatory style, which have restored in the translated poems the power in diction but no poem or the poetic appeal such as the required rhyme and limit on syllable number in the original Chinese poems. Not until the advent of Xu Yuanchong's translated poems and lyrics, was the convention of prose-style translation broken, which was a great pioneering undertaking in translating Chinese ancient poems, marking the beginning of an era for metrical, rhyming translation. Bringing translated poetry pieces infinitely closer in meaning and form to Tang poems is not only work of translation but a version of creative writing, requiring translators' great proficiency in both languages and good culture in literature.

"Prosodic translation or poetic translation" is Xu's most arresting fashion of translation and poetic thought, which has been an arduous attempt to put artistic details of the original poems into translated works. Bringing the original poems' "prosodic beauty" and "image beauty" into the translated poems, this is an act of conveying the artistic characteristics of Chinese ancient poetry to the translated poetry pieces. The "Triple Beauty" theory in poetic translation put forward by Xu Yuanchong covers "Message Beauty", "Prosodic Beauty" and "Image Beauty", through the three of which the Chinese poem's essence is thus retained in the translated poem. Nonetheless, quite a few elements of Tang poems, such as rhetorical devices, poetic images and leaving blank space, are found missing in the existing translated works, which thus deprives the English-translated poem texts of their far-reaching artistic conception and charm lying in the original text.

As Paloposki and Koskinen (2004) believe, the later translation tends to get closer to the original text than the earlier if there are two or more versions of the original text translated into the same language. Better translation of the Chinese ancient classics is the pursuit of subsequent translators, whose assiduous effort to reach a closer version of translation is the engine for the spread of Chinese classics to the West. *Tang Poems in English Rhyme* by Professor Zhao Yanchun showcases such assiduity and persistence for better translated poems. Bearing such an ambition, I am following their steps.

To make translated poem readers feel like reading a Tang poem is what we, from Professor Xu Yuanchong to Professor Zhao Yanchun and to the succeeding translators like me, yearn for and keep to, which is the voicing of our love for Chinese culture. Tang Poems that the Chinese culture gave birth to, of splendid significance and vigor, will be chanted like an enchanting song from generation to generation and sung worldwide.

Huo Hong

Feb. 29, 2024 in Yangzhou

目录 CONTENTS

野　望

王　绩

东皋薄暮望，
徒倚欲何依。
树树皆秋色，
山山唯落晖。
牧人驱犊返，
猎马带禽归。
相顾无相识，
长歌怀采薇。

A Look to the Wild

Wang Ji

At dusk, eyes on Donggao I lay,
Wondering, “I would go which way?”
From tree to tree the autumn hue,
From hill to hill th’ setting sun view.
The herdsmen drive the cattle back;
Th’ hunting horse takes home the game pack.
Each other we meet but don’t know;
“To be a recluse!” I sing so.

诗二首（其一）

王梵志

我有一方便，
价值百匹练。
相打长伏弱，
至死不入县。

Two Quatrains (No. 1)

Wang Fanzhi

I have a convenience of th' ilk,
Worth a hundred bolts of white silk.
Prostrate in fights I often lie;
Rather than see the judge I'd die.

诗二首（其二）

王梵志

他人骑大马，
我独跨驴子。
回顾担柴汉，
心下较些子。

Two Quatrains (No. 2)

Wang Fanzhi

Someone else has a horse to ride;
I have th' donkey to sit astride.
Looking back at the firewood men,
I find my heart has lifted then.

杳杳寒山道

寒 山

杳杳寒山道，
落落冷涧滨。
啾啾常有鸟，
寂寂更无人。
淅淅风吹面，
纷纷雪积身。
朝朝不见日，
岁岁不知春。

A Path up the Han Mountain Goes Far

Han Shan

A path up Han Mountain goes far;
Desolate and cold th' ravines are.
There oft chatter the birds around;
Quiet, even humans aren't found.
Rustling, to my face the winds blow;
Swirling, all over me falls th' snow.
Morn to morn, no sun's seen up there;
Year to year, of spring I'm u'aware.

蝉

虞世南

垂緌饮清露，
流响出疏桐。
居高声自远，
非是藉秋风。

Cicadas

Yu Shinan

Tentacles down, clear dew they sip;
Their chirps come from the phoenix tree.
High up, their sounds take a far trip;
Helping hands autumn winds can't be.

咏　鹅

骆宾王

鹅，鹅，鹅，
曲项向天歌，
白毛浮绿水，
红掌拨清波。

Ode to the Goose

Luo Binwang

Goose, goose, goose,
Whose neck pokes up to slur.
On green streams white plumes cruise;
Down clear waves red feet stir.

易水送别

骆宾王

此地别燕丹，
壮士发冲冠。
昔时人已没，
今日水犹寒。

Saying Farewell by the Yi River

Luo Binwang

Bidding adieu to Prince Dan here,
Jing Ke bristled up, so sincere.
Dead, the then man already goes;
Chilly, today’s river still flows.

风

李　峤

解落三秋叶，
能开二月花。
过江千尺浪，
入竹万竿斜。

The Wind

Li Qiao

It frees autumn leaves out of hold;
It can let spring flowers unfold,
Past th’ Ri’er making thousand-foot rolls,
Through bamboos bending myriad poles.

咏 风

王 勃

肃肃凉风生，
加我林壑清。
驱烟寻涧户，
卷雾出山楹。
去来固无迹，
动息如有情。
日落山水静，
为君起松声。

Ode to the Wind

Wang Bo

With soughs a cool wind does appear,
Making the trees and valley clear.
To th' riverside shacks it drives brume,
In the hill it blows out the room.
With no trace left, it comes and goes;
With th' feel received, it speeds and slows.
At sunset, hill 'nd rill go tranquil;
It rustles pines for you to th' trill.

送杜少府之任蜀州

王　勃

城阙辅三秦，
风烟望五津。
与君离别意，
同是宦游人。
海内存知己，
天涯若比邻。
无为在歧路，
儿女共沾巾。

Farewell to Mr. Du, a County Magistrate to Sichuan Province

Wang Bo

Three Qin Emperors th' town went through;
The five ferries wind and mist view.
The reason for which we depart:
We travel an official part.
There's a close friend within the sea;
Here is he who seems next to me.
It's no need: where two roads have met,
We both cry with our clothes wet.

别薛华

王 勃

送送多穷路，
遑遑独问津。
悲凉千里道，
凄断百年身。
心事同漂泊，
生涯共苦辛。
无论去与住，
俱是梦中人。

Farewell to Xue Hua

Wang Bo

I walk you as long as I may,
Worried you'll alone ask the way.
All the long journey you'll be lone;
All th' long life I'll be on my own.
Adrift are hearts of yours and mine;
Arduous is my life and thine.
Whether it is you or it's me,
The one in dreams either will be.

山 中

王 勃

长江悲已滞，
万里念将归。
况属高风晚，
山山黄叶飞。

In the Mountain

Wang Bo

By the River, I’m sad to overstay;
To th’ far home, I’m ready to make my way,
Let alone in the autumn winds that blow;
In hills and mountains fly brown leaves they throw.

渡汉江

宋之问

岭外音书断，
经冬复历春。
近乡情更怯，
不敢问来人。

Crossing the Han River

Song Zhiwen

No letters to me from home sent,
A winter and a spring I've spent.
I'm more afraid when my home's near;
To ask one who's from there I fear.

送别崔著作东征

陈子昂

金天方肃杀，
白露始专征。
王师非乐战，
之子慎佳兵。
海气侵南部，
边风扫北平。
莫卖卢龙塞，
归邀麟阁名。

Seeing Off Cui Zhu Who Goes East on Campaign

Chen Zi'ang

In Autumn chill just starts to reign;
At White Dew you go on campaign.
Wars Royal troops do not enjoy;
The force you cautiously deploy.
Like sea air, the south they invade;
Like fortress, winds the north they raid.
For your merit to never claim,
Through it you aren't to make a name.

登幽州台歌

陈子昂

前不见古人，
后不见来者。
念天地之悠悠，
独怆然而涕下！

On the Lookout of Youzhou

Chen Zi'ang

None came sages of th' past;
In future come no peers.
Thinking of heaven 'nd earth to last,
Lonely and sad, I shed my tears.

送东莱王学士无竞

陈子昂

宝剑千金买，
平生未许人。
怀君万里别，
持赠结交亲。
孤松宜晚岁，
众木爱芳春。
已矣将何道，
无令白发新。

To Wang Wujing, an Official from Donglai

Chen Zi'ang

A thousand taels the sword cost me;
None I promised to give it to.
Myriad li you will be from me;
For friendship's sake it is to you.
The lonely pine loves th' winter day;
Numerous trees enjoy spring air.
In today's world, what need I say?
Just do not have more of grey hair.

春夜别友人

陈子昂

银烛吐青烟，
金樽对绮筵。
离堂思琴瑟，
别路绕山川。
明月隐高树，
长河没晓天。
悠悠洛阳道，
此会在何年。

Farewell to a Friend on a Spring Night

Chen Zi'ang

The white candle burns with flames blue,
Gold cups glitter at th' feast all through.
We will recall the good old days;
I will wind hilly, rilly ways.
The moon screened by the tree nearby,
Th' Milky Way drowned in the dawn sky,
I'll be to Luoyang on my way;
When will be our reunion day?

感遇三十八首(其二十三)

陈子昂

翡翠巢南海，
雄雌珠树林。
何知美人意，
骄爱比黄金。
杀身炎州里，
委羽玉堂阴。
旖旎光首饰，
葳蕤烂锦衾。
岂不在遐远，
虞罗忽见寻。
多材信为累，
叹息此珍禽。

Thirty-eight Observations (No. 23)

Chen Zi'ang

The jade bird nests by Southern Seas;
In pairs they fly up and down trees.
How can you know the view belles hold,
To treasure them as much as gold?
In th' tropical zone they're slayed;
In the court their plumage is laid.
The feathers make ornaments shine;
Quilts graced with plumage appear fine.
Do they not reside far away?
Now found and now captured are they.
Their merit causes them to die;
Over the precious bird I sigh.

晚次乐乡县

陈子昂

故乡杳无际，
日暮且孤征。
川原迷旧国，
道路入边城。
野戍荒烟断，
深山古木平。
如何此时恨，
嗷嗷夜猿鸣。

Putting Up for the Night in Lexiang County

Chen Zi'ang

Far, my hometown is out of sight;
I'm on th' lone trip with th' fall of night.
Hills and rills conduct the way down;
Roads 'nd paths lead to a border town.
Th' post tower and wild mist not found,
Mountains and trees level with th' ground,
Why am I at this hour so blue?
At night apes howl and so they do.

回乡偶书（其一）

贺知章

少小离家老大回，
乡音无改鬓毛衰。
儿童相见不相识，
笑问客从何处来。

Ode to Homecoming (No. 1)

He Zhizhang

Leaving home young, I returned an old he,
My home accent unchanged, my hair had thinned.
A few children came up not knowing me;
"Where in the world do you come from?" they grinned.

回乡偶书(其二)

贺知章

离别家乡岁月多，
近来人事半消磨。
唯有门前镜湖水，
春风不改旧时波。

Ode to Homecoming（No. 2）

He Zhizhang

For an aeon from hometown I was away;
Lately things have altered many a way.
It's just Mirror Lake water before th' gate
That the spring winds don't change the waves' old state.

咏　柳

贺知章

碧玉妆成一树高，
万条垂下绿丝绦。
不知细叶谁裁出，
二月春风似剪刀。

Ode to the Willow

He Zhizhang

The willow trees get attired in jade green;
Thousands of wickers droop in silky sheen.
You wonder who's tailored thin leaves so clean;
Scissors th' second lunar month winds have been.

题袁氏别业

贺知章

主人不相识，
偶坐为林泉。
莫谩愁沽酒，
囊中自有钱。

Dedication to Yuan's Villa

He Zhizhang

The garden's owner I don't know;
To sit for woods and springs I go.
Don't worry over buying wine;
I have taels in th' pocket of mine.

闺 怨

沈如筠

雁尽书难寄，
愁多梦不成。
愿随孤月影，
流照伏波营。

A Wife's Lament

Shen Ruyun

Wild geese gone, letters I can't send;
With sorrow, sleep doesn't descend.
The moonlight, with which she would go,
Shining o'er his barracks, will flow.

赋得自君之出矣

张九龄

自君之出矣，
不复理残机。
思君如满月，
夜夜减清辉。

Since You Went Away

Zhang Jiuling

Since you went away from home then,
I haven’t worked the loom again.
Missing you, I’m like th’ full moon bright,
Whose light dims away night by night.

感　遇(其七)

张九龄

江南有丹橘，
经冬犹绿林。
岂伊地气暖？
自有岁寒心。
可以荐嘉客，
奈何阻重深。
运命惟所遇，
循环不可寻。
徒言树桃李，
此木岂无阴？

Observations (No. 7)

Zhang Jiuling

In South Land there grows th' tangerine;
Through the winter it remains green.
How can it be for the warmth there?
By nature cold the tree can bear.
Whose fruit you can so recommend,
Which but has a hard way to wend.
Fate is a chance to meet and hold,
The law of which cannot be told.
Only peaches and plums are grown;
Can't this tree have shade of its own?

望月怀远

张九龄

海上生明月，
天涯共此时。
情人怨遥夜，
竟夕起相思。
灭烛怜光满，
披衣觉露滋。
不堪盈手赠，
还寝梦佳期。

A Recollection of Those Far Away during the Moon Watching

Zhang Jiuling

Bright, th' moon rises over the sea;
Far away, you share it with me.
Th' loving one groans for the night long;
He stays up the night all along.
Th' candle out, he loves the moon's light;
With a coat on, he feels th' chill slight.
He can't pass with his hands the view,
But goes back to sleep to meet you.

登鹳雀楼

王之涣

白日依山尽，
黄河入海流。
欲穷千里目，
更上一层楼。

Ascending the Stork Tower

Wang Zhihuan

Down the mountain the sun does go;
In th' sea th' Yellow River does flow.
Meaning to have a broadest view,
One should ascend a flight anew.

宴 词

王之涣

长堤春水绿悠悠，
畎入漳河一道流。
莫听声声催去棹，
桃溪浅处不胜舟。

A Farewell Poem Composed at the Banquet

Wang Zhihuan

Far is the dike and the green spring rills go;
Ditches join th' Zhang River and on they flow.
Listen not to th' oars urging you aboard;
The Peach Stream can't run the boat at the ford.

凉州词

王之涣

黄河远上白云间，
一片孤城万仞山。
羌笛何须怨杨柳，
春风不度玉门关。

Ode to Liangzhou City

Wang Zhihuan

The Yellow River flows down from the sky;
Along are a lone town and mountains high.
Why play *The Willows* on Qiang flute in woe?
Past Yumen Gate vernal winds never blow.

早寒江上有怀

孟浩然

木落雁南度，
北风江上寒。
我家襄水曲，
遥隔楚云端。
乡泪客中尽，
孤帆天际看。
迷津欲有问，
平海夕漫漫。

A Lyric on the Cold River

Meng Haoran

As leaves fall, to th' south wild geese trill;
North winds bring over th' river chill.
I lived near the Xiang River's bend,
My home lies at the Chu's clouds' end.
Here homesick tears of mine run dry;
A lone sail in sight roams the sky.
The way to the port I don't know;
Calm and vast, th' dusk water does flow.

春　晓

孟浩然

春眠不觉晓，
处处闻啼鸟。
夜来风雨声，
花落知多少。

A Spring Daybreak

Meng Haoran

Day breaks while I sleep unaware;
I hear birds twitter here and there.
Last night wind and rain made a sound.
How many flowers fall aground?

宿桐庐江寄广陵旧游

孟浩然

山暝听猿愁，
沧江急夜流。
风鸣两岸叶，
月照一孤舟。
建德非吾土，
维扬忆旧游。
还将两行泪，
遥寄海西头。

A Sentiment to Old Friends in Yangzhou from My Putting Up at the Tonglu River

Meng Haoran

Th' hills dim, the apes' cries make me grieve;
In the night flies the river blue.
Winds rustle the on-the-bank leave;
The moon lights up a lone canoe.
Jiande's not where home is at all;
Yangzhou's where old friends I miss are,
The two lines of my tears that fall,
To the west of th' sea I'll send far.

宿建德江

孟浩然

移舟泊烟渚，
日暮客愁新。
野旷天低树，
江清月近人。

Putting Up on the Jiande River

Meng Haoran

Off th' misty isle my boat I draw;
The fall of night brought one more sore.
Wild land vast, skies come below th' tree;
The river clear, th' moon lies by me.

望秦川

李 颀

秦川朝望迥，
日出正东峰。
远近山河净，
逶迤城阙重。
秋声万户竹，
寒色五陵松。
客有归欤叹，
凄其霜露浓。

Looking Back to the Qin Plains

Li Qi

At dawn the Qin Plains far to eyes,
Over th' east peak the sun does rise.
Hills and rills run clear far and near;
The town walls wind their way in tier.
Autumn winds sound doors and bamboo;
The five tombs pines wear a cold hue.
I sigh over my leaving will;
Thick is the frost and dew—so chill.

采莲曲

王昌龄

荷叶罗裙一色裁，
芙蓉向脸两边开。
乱入池中看不见，
闻歌始觉有人来。

The Tune of Collecting Lotuses

Wang Changling

Tinged with lotus leaves, the skirt comes so green;
Lotuses open, the face comes between.
Mid the lotuses, she escapes the eye;
Hearing the song, I know one's coming by.

芙蓉楼送辛渐

王昌龄

寒雨连江夜入吴，
平明送客楚山孤。
洛阳亲友如相问，
一片冰心在玉壶。

Seeing Off Xin Jian at the Furong Tower

Wang Changling

Chill rain joined the River to Wu at night,
At dawn you left Mount Chu, ’nd I alone stayed.
If relatives ’nd friends ask if I’m all right,
My heart is like ice in a vase of jade.

闺怨

王昌龄

闺中少妇不知愁，
春日凝妆上翠楼。
忽见陌头杨柳色，
悔教夫婿觅封侯。

A Wife's Lament

Wang Changling

Carefree, the young wife in th' boudoir has been;
On a spring day, dressed up, upstairs she gets.
Willow green she of a sudden has seen;
Bidding her man to seek ranks she regrets.

答武陵太守

王昌龄

仗剑行千里，
微躯感一言。
曾为大梁客，
不负信陵恩。

A Reply to Prefect of Wuling

Wang Changling

I'll go a thousand li with th' sword;
Pray let me have a word to say:
I once served, you being my lord;
Your trust I will never betray.

送柴侍御

王昌龄

沅水通波接武冈，
送君不觉有离伤。
青山一道同云雨，
明月何曾是两乡。

Farewell to Mr. Chai

Wang Changling

The Yuan River flows to Mound Wu at all;
Seeing you off, I am not feeling blue.
Over th' mound the same clouds come and rains fall;
Under the moon, how can one town be two?

出　塞

王昌龄

秦时明月汉时关，
万里长征人未还。
但使龙城飞将在，
不教胡马度阴山。

Beyond the Great Wall

Wang Changling

The moon and the pass as of yore remain;
There soldiers on th' myriad-li march have lain.
If in post th' Loong Town general were set,
Over Mount Yin no Hu steeds would be let.

终南望余雪

祖 咏

终南阴岭秀，
积雪浮云端。
林表明霁色，
城中增暮寒。

Watching the Unmelted Snow

Zu Yong

Th’ north of th’ mountain has a fine sight;
Unmelted snow lies at cloud height.
The forest glows after the snow;
Dusk sees cold of the city grow.

相　思

王　维

红豆生南国，
春来发几枝。
愿君多采撷，
此物最相思。

A Feeling of Missing

Wang Wei

In Southern Land red beans abound;
In spring many shoot above ground.
May you pick and collect a host;
The thing makes you miss me the most.

山居秋暝

王　维

空山新雨后，
天气晚来秋。
明月松间照，
清泉石上流。
竹喧归浣女，
莲动下渔舟。
随意春芳歇，
王孙自可留。

The Autumn Sight of the Hills at Nightfall

Wang Wei

Vast and quiet are after-rain hills;
As night comes the autumn hue grows.
Through the pines the bright moonlight spills;
Over the stones the clear creek flows.
Washing girls back, th' bamboo dinned loud;
Boats coming down, th' lily pads sway.
To just go by spring is allowed;
I myself may have a long stay.

书　事

王　维

轻阴阁小雨，
深院昼慵开。
坐看苍苔色，
欲上人衣来。

A Poem on the Immediate Sight

Wang Wei

It's cloudy after a light rain;
To open th' yard gate I'm not fain.
I sit and watch the moss so green
That to my clothes green has been.

送元二使安西

王　维

渭城朝雨浥轻尘，
客舍青青柳色新。
劝君更尽一杯酒，
西出阳关无故人。

Seeing Off Yuan'er to Anxi

Wang Wei

Wei Town's ground dirt wets with a morning rain;
The inn green mid fresh colour willows gain.
My friend, drink up another cup of wine;
West of Sun Pass you'll have no friend of thine.

竹里馆

王　维

独坐幽篁里，
弹琴复长啸。
深林人不知，
明月来相照。

A Cottage among Bamboos

Wang Wei

Alone among bamboos I stay,
Playing strings and singing away.
No one knows in th’ deep grove I’ve been;
Over me a bright moon does sheen.

九月九日忆山东兄弟

王　维

独在异乡为异客，
每逢佳节倍思亲。
遥知兄弟登高处，
遍插茱萸少一人。

Ode to the Missing of My Brothers East of Mt. Hua on the Ninth of the Ninth Moon

Wang Wei

I a visitor dwell in a strange land;
Homesickness at Festivals does expand.
From far I know my brothers climb a mound,
Who wear cornel sprigs without one around.

山中送别

王　维

山中相送罢，
日暮掩柴扉。
春草明年绿，
王孙归不归。

Seeing Off My Friend in the Hills

Wang Wei

In th' hills I see you off on th' tour;
At dusk I close the wicket door.
Next spring grass will turn green again;
Will you come back to me by then?

陇西行

王 维

十里一走马，
五里一扬鞭。
都护军书至，
匈奴围酒泉。
关山正飞雪，
烽火断无烟。

A Trip to the West of Gansu Province

Wang Wei

Ten li covered on the horse run,
Five li covered with a whip done,
Word from the governor comes then
That Jiuquan's besieged by th' Hun men.
Over the mountain pass flies snow;
From th' beacons comes no smoky glow.

过香积寺

王　维

不知香积寺，
数里入云峰。
古木无人径，
深山何处钟。
泉声咽危石，
日色冷青松。
薄暮空潭曲，
安禅制毒龙。

A Visit to Xiangji Temple

Wang Wei

Where the temple is I don't know.
To th' cloud-wreathed peak for miles I go.
On old-tree-lined trails is no soul;
Through the deep mountain comes the toll.
Against stones the creek sobs and whines;
Through the pines the sun chills and shines.
As on the quiet vast pool night falls,
Buddhist sit holds back earthly calls.

山 中

王 维

荆溪白石出，
天寒红叶稀。
山路元无雨，
空翠湿人衣。

In the Hill

Wang Wei

When th' Jingxi Rill flows, white stones spill;
As it goes chill, sparse red leaves get.
In fact there's no rain in the hill;
With th' vastness of green my coat's wet.

使至塞上

王　维

单车欲问边，
属国过居延。
征蓬出汉塞，
归雁入胡天。
大漠孤烟直，
长河落日圆。
萧关逢候骑，
都护在燕然。

On Mission beyond the Great Wall

Wang Wei

To inspect th' frontier in a single drive,
At th' vassal state of Juyan I arrive.
Over the Fortress thistledown gets by;
Into the Hu's sky wild geese fly north high.
The wild sees winds whirl up straight from aground;
The River witnesses th' sun set down round.
At Xiao Pass camp I meet a riding scout,
Who says at Yanran th' general's about.

画

王 维

远看山有色，
近听水无声。
春去花还在，
人来鸟不惊。

A Painting

Wang Wei

Seen from far, hills have a hued glow;
Heard from near, rills flow a hushed flow.
Gone as spring is, still blossoms stay;
Though men come, birds aren't scared away.

鹿 柴

王 维

空山不见人，
但闻人语响。
返景入深林，
复照青苔上。

At Luzhai

Wang Wei

In mountains no one’s seen aground;
There some voices are heard around.
In the deep woods come the sun’s rays;
Upon the moss they make their ways.

杂诗三首(其二)

王 维

君自故乡来，
应知故乡事。
来日绮窗前，
寒梅著花未。

Miscellaneous Poems (No. 2)

Wang Wei

From my very hometown thou art;
What's happened thither you must know.
At th' window when you did depart,
Did the wintersweet there yet blow?

少年行(其一)

王 维

新丰美酒斗十千，
咸阳游侠多少年。
相逢意气为君饮，
系马高楼垂柳边。

A Trip of the Young Man's (No. 1)

Wang Wei

Ten thousand taels is each cup of good wine,
Swordsmen in Xianyang are mostly young guys.
One meets, finds them congenial and drinks fine,
His steed by th' tower to willows he ties.

少年行(其二)

王 维

出身仕汉羽林郎，
初随骠骑战渔阳。
孰知不向边庭苦，
纵死犹闻侠骨香。

A Trip of the Young Man's (No. 2)

Wang Wei

For the Royal Guard I had ever wrought,
'Nd after General to Yuyang first fought.
The pain of no border serving who knows?
The hero's scent death in the battles sows.

少年行（其三）

王 维

一身能擘两雕弧，
虏骑千重只似无。
偏坐金鞍调白羽，
纷纷射杀五单于。

A Trip of the Young Man’s (No. 3)

Wang Wei

Two bows at a time he could draw,
With th’ foe cavalry to ignore.
Over th’ saddle setting th’ arrow,
He shot the five chiefs in a row.

少年行(其四)

王　维

汉家君臣欢宴终，
高议云台论战功。
天子临轩赐侯印，
将军佩出明光宫。

A Trip of the Young Man's (No. 4)

Wang Wei

To an end th' monarch-subject feast did go;
At th' platform battle feats were talked about.
Th' king stepped forth, a marquis seal to bestow;
Th' general wore it, the court to get out.

闲 居

王 维

桃红复含宿雨，
柳绿更带朝烟。
花落家童未扫，
莺啼山客犹眠。

A Leisurely Life

Wang Wei

Last night's rain peach blossoms still snare;
Morning's mist willow leaves just bear.
Blooms fallen, th' boy servants don't sweep,
Orioles chirping, th' recluses sleep.

左掖梨花

丘为

冷艳全欺雪，
余香乍入衣。
春风且莫定，
吹向玉阶飞。

Pear Blossoms on the Left

Qiu Wei

That of snow their cool brightness beats;
Clothes their lingering scent meets.
Spring winds, don’t stay still coming by,
Blow to the steps and make them fly.

沐浴子

李　白

沐芳莫弹冠，
浴兰莫振衣。
处世忌太洁，
至人贵藏晖。
沧浪有钓叟，
吾与尔同归。

The Bath-taker

Li Bai

Washing hair, your cap you don't tap;
Bathing, your garment you don't flap.
You quit being too clean on earth;
A great man knows to hide his worth.
An old fisherman's mid waves blue;
Around the world I'll follow you.

赠汪伦

李 白

李白乘舟将欲行，
忽闻岸上踏歌声。
桃花潭水深千尺，
不及汪伦送我情。

To Wang Lun

Li Bai

By boat Li Bai's about to go along.
Heard suddenly, from the bank treads a song.
The Peach Pond's deep, a thousand feet to be;
Not as deep as Wang Lun's friendship to me.

送友人

李　白

青山横北郭，
白水绕东城。
此地一为别，
孤蓬万里征。
浮云游子意，
落日故人情。
挥手自兹去，
萧萧班马鸣。

Seeing Off a Friend

Li Bai

North of town green mountains sit by;
East of town clear water winds past.
Here we bid each other goodbye;
Th' thistledown drifts a distance vast.
Your heart a floating cloud does show;
Our friendship th' setting sun does say.
Waving your hand, from here you go;
His saddle horse neighs a loud neigh.

鲁郡东石门送杜二甫

李　白

醉别复几日，
登临遍池台。
何时石门路，
重有金樽开。
秋波落泗水，
海色明徂徕。
飞蓬各自远，
且尽手中杯。

Seeing Off Du Fu at Mt. Stone Gate East of Shandong Province

Li Bai

In the days to part, days we spend;
Pools approached, towers we ascend.
When'll we meet at Mt. Stone Gate then?
To drain cups together again.
Th' Si River rolls, fall waves to be;
Mt. Culai sheens, greened by the sea.
To th' distance th' thistledown blown up,
Why do we not raise 'nd finish th' cup?

下终南山
过斛斯山人宿置酒

李　白

暮从碧山下，
山月随人归。
却顾所来径，
苍苍横翠微。
相携及田家，
童稚开荆扉。
绿竹入幽径，
青萝拂行衣。
欢言得所憩，
美酒聊共挥。
长歌吟松风，
曲尽河星稀。
我醉君复乐，
陶然共忘机。

A Call at Recluse Husi' s Home and Drinking with Him down the Zhongnan Mountain

Li Bai

At dusk the mountain I descend;
The moon overhead follows me.
I turn round to see th' way I wend,
All green across th' mountain to be.
Along with him I'm to his home;
His child opens the wicket door.
The path amid bamboos I roam;
Clothes of passers-by th' vines draw.
Let's chat and have some rest along;
Let's raise and drink good cups of wine.
Wind through the Pines, we sing the song;
The song over, stars have lost shine.
I'm drunk, which makes him give a smile;
In joy we leave behind all guile.

哭宣城善酿纪叟

李　白

纪叟黄泉里，
还应酿老春。
夜台无晓日，
沽酒与何人。

Crying over Mr. Ji, an Old Man Good at Brewing Wine in Xuancheng

Li Bai

In the netherworld now you fare;
You must be still brewing your wine.
There's never daybreak over there;
To whom do you sell wine of thine?

或

In th' netherworld you fare;
The old wine you still brew.
Day never breaks in there.
Whom do you sell it to?

劳劳亭

李　白

天下伤心处，
劳劳送客亭。
春风知别苦，
不遣柳条青。

The Laolao Bower

Li Bai

The place does break one's heart,
Th' bower where off one's seen.
Spring winds know th' woe to part,
Not to get th' willows green.

访戴天山道士不遇

李　白

犬吠水声中，
桃花带露浓。
树深时见鹿，
溪午不闻钟。
野竹分青霭，
飞泉挂碧峰。
无人知所去，
愁倚两三松。

A Call on the Monk at Mount Daitian in Vain

Li Bai

With dogs' barks and the water flow,
The peach blossoms carry thick dew.
In th' deep woods, deer oft come and go;
To the noon's creek, no toll comes through.
Mid wild bamboos blue mist does break;
Down the green peak water does fly.
No one knows for where he would make;
Against the pines I'm sad to lie.

谢公亭

李　白

谢亭离别处，
风景每生愁。
客散青天月，
山空碧水流。
池花春映日，
窗竹夜鸣秋。
今古一相接，
长歌怀旧游。

Master Xie Tower

Li Bai

The tower's a place to depart;
Each sight of it just breaks my heart.
Friends gone, the moon in th' blue sky shows;
The hills void , the green water flows.
On pool-side blooms th' spring sun shines bright;
In fall the night bamboo soughs right.
Past and present are joined along;
For their old trip I sing a song.

登金陵凤凰台

李　白

凤凰台上凤凰游，
凤去台空江自流。
吴宫花草埋幽径，
晋代衣冠成古丘。
三山半落青天外，
二水中分白鹭洲。
总为浮云能蔽日，
长安不见使人愁。

Ascending Phoenix Terrace in Jinling

Li Bai

To Phoenix Terrace, the phoenix a guest,
The bird gone, terrace void, th' River streams still.
In the path Wu's palace blooms and grass rest,
Coats 'nd hat of Jin Dynasty turns small hill.
Half to the sky,the San Mountain does run;
Egret Isle amid th' Qinhuai, two rills flow.
Floating clouds overhead eclipse the sun;
To visit Chang'an I'm sad not to go.

静夜思

李 白

床前明月光，
疑是地上霜。
举头望明月，
低头思故乡。

A Thought on a Tranquil Night

Li Bai

Before the well rests the moon’s light,
Which is thought to be frost aground.
Head up, I see the moon so bright;
Head down, I find my mind home-bound.

山中与幽人对酌

李 白

两人对酌山花开，
一杯一杯复一杯。
我醉欲眠聊且去，
明朝有意抱琴来。

Drinking with Recluse in the Mountains

Li Bai

Amid the full blooms drink two men;
After one cup is one more then.
Drunk, I'm to sleep and off you'll be;
Come next morn with the lute to me.

将进酒

李　白

君不见，
黄河之水天上来，
奔流到海不复回。
君不见，
高堂明镜悲白发，
朝如青丝暮成雪。
人生得意须尽欢，
莫使金樽空对月。
天生我材必有用，
千金散尽还复来。
烹羊宰牛且为乐，
会须一饮三百杯。

岑夫子，丹丘生，
将进酒，杯莫停。
与君歌一曲，
请君为我倾耳听。
钟鼓馔玉不足贵，
但愿长醉不愿醒。
古来圣贤皆寂寞，
惟有饮者留其名。
陈王昔时宴平乐，
斗酒十千恣欢谑。

主人何为言少钱，
径须沽取对君酌。
五花马，千金裘，
呼儿将出换美酒，
与尔同销万古愁。

Please Drink

Li Bai

Cannot you see,
Th' Yellow River comes from the sky,
Runs to the sea, back it won't fly.
Cannot you see,
Parents' hair gray, the bronze makes woe;
Morn finds it black silk and dusk snow.
When pleased, one has a best time up;
Don't hold to the moon just a cup.
A talent of use in my vein,
Ingots spent up I will regain.
With lamb and beef served, I have fun;
At one go I would drink a ton.

Cen Xun and Dan Qiu friends of mine
Just hold up cups and drink the wine.
I will sing you a song;
Please listen to me all along.
Bells, drums and dainties are not dear;
May I be drunk, my head not clear.
Lonely is the sage from of old;
A name only the drinkers hold.
Prince Chen oft holds palace feasts then,
Drank barrels, and had fun again.
Why claim I pay less to the host?
Go buy wine and we'll drink the most.
My dapple steed, fur worth much gold,
Call the boy to sell them for wine;
With them I'll be off woe of mine.

黄鹤楼送孟浩然之广陵

李　白

故人西辞黄鹤楼，
烟花三月下扬州。
孤帆远影碧空尽，
唯见长江天际流。

Seeing Off Meng Haoran to Guangling at Yellow Crane Tower

Li Bai

He leaves th' Yellow Crane Tower, my old friend;
In March of catkins to Yangzhou he'll go.
His lone sail's vanished where the sky does end;
In sight to th' horizon, th' River does flow.

秋浦歌(其十四)

李 白

炉火照天地，
红星乱紫烟。
赧郎明月夜，
歌曲动寒川。

A Song of the Autumn Riverside (No. 14)

Li Bai

Th’ furnace lights between th’ earth and sky;
Sparks crack into purple smoke high.
The fire-lit men make the night gleam;
Their song makes the cold river stream.

秋浦歌(其十五)

李 白

白发三千丈，
缘愁似个长。
不知明镜里，
何处得秋霜。

A Song of the Autumn Riverside (No. 15)

Li Bai

Long long my hair does grow,
For long long runs my woe.
I don’t know in th’ bronze bright
How I get a frost bite.

早发白帝城

李 白

朝辞白帝彩云间，
千里江陵一日还。
两岸猿声啼不住，
轻舟已过万重山。

Early Departure from Baidi Town

Li Bai

At dawn I leave Baidi mid th' rosy cloud;
It's a day's ride to Jiangling down the rills.
The apes from both banks cry non-stop cries loud;
The skiff travels down past ten thousand hills.

望天门山

李　白

天门中断楚江开，
碧水东流至此回。
两岸青山相对出，
孤帆一片日边来。

Watching Mt. Tianmen

Li Bai

The Chu River cuts Mt. Tianmen apart;
Green flows go east and here makes a back dart.
Green mountains on both banks come face to face;
A lonely sail filled comes from the sun's place.

夜泊牛渚怀古

李　白

牛渚西江夜，
青天无片云。
登舟望秋月，
空忆谢将军。
余亦能高咏，
斯人不可闻。
明朝挂帆席，
枫叶落纷纷。

Night Mooring at Isle Niu

Li Bai

At Isle Niu mid the West River at night,
With no single cloud in the sky,
On board the autumn moon I sight;
The thought of Marshal Xie drops by.
Sing loud I myself also can,
But this man cannot hear my song.
To set sail morrow morn I plan;
The maple leaves twirl down along.

月下独酌四首(其一)

李 白

花间一壶酒，
独酌无相亲。
举杯邀明月，
对影成三人。
月既不解饮，
影徒随我身。
暂伴月将影，
行乐须及春。
我歌月徘徊，
我舞影零乱。
醒时同交欢，
醉后各分散。
永结无情游，
相期邈云汉。

Drinking Alone under the Moon (No. 1)

Li Bai

A bottle of wine amid blooms,
I drink alone, and no kin looms.
Raising my cup, th' moon I invite;
Th' shadow makes threes persons in sight.
A drinker the moon cannot be;
The shadow only follows me.
For th' moment, I stay with the two;
To have fun, I pass spring all through.
While I sing, the moon hangs around;
While I dance, th' shadow is not found.
Sober, we both enjoy our play;
Tipsy, we each go our own way.
Without friendship, we'll be drawn nigh;
We will meet in the misty sky.

望庐山瀑布

李　白

日照香炉生紫烟，
遥看瀑布挂前川。
飞流直下三千尺，
疑是银河落九天。

Watching Lushan Mountain Waterfall

Li Bai

Th' sun lights Peak Censer spraying purple steam;
I see from far the fall pouring a stream.
From a thousand metres the stream does fly,
Thought to be the Milky Way from the sky.

自遣

李白

对酒不觉暝，
落花盈我衣。
醉起步溪月，
鸟还人亦稀。

A Distraction of Mine

Li Bai

I don’t know it is dark with wine;
Fallen blooms strew the gown of mine.
Sobered, down th’ moon-lit stream I roam;
Men rarely seen, birds return home.

夜宿山寺

李　白

危楼高百尺，
手可摘星辰。
不敢高声语，
恐惊天上人。

Putting Up for the Night at a Mountain Temple

Li Bai

The tower's a hundred feet high,
On which to pick stars one may try.
One doesn't dare speak in a cry,
Afraid to disturb those in th's sky.

客中行

李 白

兰陵美酒郁金香，
玉碗盛来琥珀光。
但使主人能醉客，
不知何处是他乡。

My Sojourn

Li Bai

Strong, golden, and sweet is good Lanling wine;
Looking amber in jade bowls, it does shine.
With the wine, drunk the host's ever made me;
That here is not hometown I do not see.

独坐敬亭山

李　白

众鸟高飞尽，
孤云独去闲。
相看两不厌，
只有敬亭山。

Sitting Alone Opposite Mt. Jingting

Li Bai

A flock of birds soar out of sight;
A lone cloud roam away in flight.
We face each other, neither tired;
To me Mt. Jingting's but required.

渡荆门送别

李　白

渡远荆门外，
来从楚国游。
山随平野尽，
江入大荒流。
月下飞天镜，
云生结海楼。
仍怜故乡水，
万里送行舟。

Farewell at Mt. Jingmen

Li Bai

I come from far to Mt. Jingmen
For a travel in the Chu State.
At the great plain the mountains end;
To the vast wild th' River does wend.
A stream mirror the moon has laid;
A mirage tower clouds have made.
Beloved home water streams her way,
'Nd sees my boat off from far away.

今夜洛城闻笛

李　白

谁家玉笛暗飞声，
散入春风满洛城。
此夜曲中闻折柳，
何人不起故园情。

A Flute Heard in Luoyang Tonight

Li Bai

From whose jade flute a song through the air creeps;
With spring winds all over Luoyang it sweeps.
Tonight to me *Snapping the Willow* flies;
Whose nostalgia will not at all arise?

上三峡

李　白

巫山夹青山，
巴水流若兹。
巴水忽可尽，
青天无到时。
三朝上黄牛，
三暮行太迟。
三朝又三暮，
不觉鬓成丝。

Up the Three Gorges

Li Bai

The sky rests in th' Wu Mountain's hold;
Like this th' Ba Water waves have rolled.
Of a sudden the river ends;
Always to skies the way extends.
Three morns round Huangniu Gorge I stay;
Three evenings upstream I delay.
Three morns and three evenings I go;
Ere I know silk side hair does grow.

闻王昌龄左迁龙标遥有此寄

李　白

杨花落尽子规啼，
闻道龙标过五溪。
我寄愁心与明月，
随君直到夜郎西。

A Word Sent to Wang Changling on His Demotion to Longbiao

Li Bai

Catkins gone, cuckoos' calls come to the ear;
You passed the five Streams to Longbiao, I hear.
To the moon I send my sorrowful heart;
To the west of Yelang with you it'll dart.

春　思

李　白

燕草如碧丝，
秦桑低绿枝。
当君怀归日，
是妾断肠时。
春风不相识，
何事入罗帏？

A Thought in Spring

Li Bai

Like the silk thread Yan's grass does grow;
Their twigs bent Qin's mulberries make.
The day you think of home to go,
Th' time I guess of my heart to break.
An acquaintance spring wind's not been;
Why do you come through the bed screen?

行路难

李 白

金樽清酒斗十千，
玉盘珍羞直万钱。
停杯投箸不能食，
拔剑四顾心茫然。
欲渡黄河冰塞川，
将登太行雪满山。
闲来垂钓碧溪上，
忽复乘舟梦日边。
行路难，行路难，
多歧路，今安在？
长风破浪会有时，
直挂云帆济沧海。

Hard Is the Way!

Li Bai

Worth ten thousand ingots is the cupped wine;
Worth myriad taels are dainties on plates fine.
Dropping cup ’nd chopsticks, diner I can’t be:
I draw my sword and look around, at sea.
I’m to cross th’ Yellow Ri’er, stopped by iced rills;
I’m to climb Mt. Taihang, blocked by snow hills.
In my free time, I fish by a green stream,
Or go towards th’ sun by boat in a dream.
Hard is the way! Hard is the way!
Many astray, how’s yours today?
There will be time to ride winds and break waves;
Sail set up high, I’ll cross the sea that raves.

怨　情

李　白

美人卷珠帘，
深坐颦蛾眉。
但见泪痕湿，
不知心恨谁？

A Lament

Li Bai

A beauty rolls up the bead screen,
Sitting long, her brow knitted so.
Her cheeks wet with tears only seen,
Whom does she hate—no one does know.

移家别湖上亭

戎昱

好是春风湖上亭，
柳条藤蔓系离情。
黄莺久住浑相识，
欲别频啼四五声。

Farewell to the Lake Pavillion as I Move House

Rong Yu

The lake pavilion in spring winds is fine;
Parting woe lies in wickers and the vine.
All orioles that have lived here long I know;
They let out four or five cries as I go.

霁雪

戎昱

风卷寒云暮雪晴，
江烟洗尽柳条轻。
檐前数片无人扫，
又得书窗一夜明。

Clearing Up after the Snow

Rong Yu

Clouds blown off, it's clear after last night's snow;
Rill mist washed away, lithe willow twigs grow.
The open spaces by the eaves stay white,
Light through the study window one more night.

黄鹤楼

崔　颢

昔人已乘黄鹤去，
此地空余黄鹤楼。
黄鹤一去不复返，
白云千载空悠悠。
晴川历历汉阳树，
芳草萋萋鹦鹉洲。
日暮乡关何处是？
烟波江上使人愁。

The Yellow Crane Tower

Cui Hao

The sage's away on his yellow crane,
The Yellow Crane Tower's left to remain.
Th' yellow crane will never return once gone;
Mere white clouds will for aeons stay on and on.
By th' Sun River the eye-catching trees stand;
On Parrot Shoal lush green grass does expand.
Where my hometown is, the night cannot show;
The mist over th' river brings me to woe.

宿云门寺阁

孙 逖

香阁东山下，
烟花象外幽。
悬灯千嶂夕，
卷幔五湖秋。
画壁馀鸿雁，
纱窗宿斗牛。
更疑天路近，
梦与白云游。

Putting Up at Yunmen Fane

Sun Ti

At th' foot of Mt. East sits the fane;
Beyond the flowers peace has lain.
Lamps hung, a thousand peaks run clear;
Screens rolled, Five Lake's autumn comes here.
On the fresco the wild goose flies;
On the window the starlight lies.
I bet the way skywards draws nigh,
Dreaming with clouds I roam the sky.

别董大(其一)

高 适

千里黄云白日曛，
北风吹雁雪纷纷。
莫愁前路无知己，
天下谁人不识君。

Farewell to Dong Da (No. 1)

Gao Shi

In the thousand-li-distance dusky skies,
In north winds snow after the wild goose flies.
Do not fear no close friend you will have got;
My bosom friend, whoever knows you not?

别董大(其二)

高　适

六翮飘飘私自怜，
一离京洛十余年。
丈夫贫贱应未足，
今日相逢无酒钱。

Farewell to Dong Da (No. 2)

Gao Shi

Self-pitied, a bird’s drifting life I lead;
From th’ two towns, over ten years I’m away.
A lowly poor life meets not a man’s need;
We meet today but for th’ wine I can’t pay.

逢雪宿芙蓉山主人

刘长卿

日暮苍山远，
天寒白屋贫。
柴门闻犬吠，
风雪夜归人。

Taking Shelter from a Snow at Mt. Furong

Liu Zhangqing

The mountains loom far in the dark;
A shack seems poor on a cold day.
Out the wood gate comes the dog's bark;
On th' snowy night one's back this way.

听弹琴

刘长卿

泠泠七弦上，
静听松风寒。
古调虽自爱，
今人多不弹。

Listening to the Lute

Liu Zhangqing

Clearly played on the seven strings,
Listened to, *Wind through Pines* feels cold.
I'm myself fond of the tune old;
Seldom played now, it hardly rings.

送灵澈上人

刘长卿

苍苍竹林寺，
杳杳钟声晚。
荷笠带斜阳，
青山独归远。

Seeing Off the Monk Lingche

Liu Zhangqing

The temple in th' grove of bamboo,
From far the evening toll comes through.
In th' bamboo hat, as the sun sets,
Back to the hill, further he gets.

秋日登吴公台上寺远眺

刘长卿

古台摇落后，
秋日望乡心。
野寺人来少，
云峰水隔深。
夕阳依旧垒，
寒磬满空林。
惆怅南朝事，
长江独至今。

Looking into the Distance at the Wugong Temple on an Autumn Day

Liu Zhangqing

Th' ancient platform does sway and fall,
Homesickness brought by th' autumn day.
At the remote temple few call;
Across the water clouds do stay.
Against th' platform th' setting sun's cast;
Through the empty wood the toll goes.
I am sad about what has passed;
To now only the Yangtze flows.

送上人

刘长卿

孤云将野鹤，
岂向人间住。
莫买沃洲山，
时人已知处。

Seeing Off the Monk

Liu Zhangqing

A lone cloud and wild crane of grace,
How can you dwell in mortals' place,
To Mount Wozhou you never go;
A recluse's point th' public know.

曲江对酒(其一)

杜 甫

一片花飞减却春，
风飘万点正愁人。
且看欲尽花经眼，
莫厌伤多酒入唇。
江上小楼巢翡翠，
苑边高冢卧麒麟。
细推物理须行乐，
何用浮名绊此身。

Drinking, Face toward the Bending Pool (No. 1)

Du Fu

Spring loses its colour as blossoms fly;
Myriad petals in the wind make me pine.
Do watch the blooms as they waft past the eye;
Mind not your much sadness while you drink wine.
In the riverside tower halcyons nest;
By the tomb a stone kylin lies aside.
In reason we should enjoy ourselves best;
Why by ranks or fame ought we to be tied?

春 望

杜 甫

国破山河在，
城春草木深。
感时花溅泪，
恨别鸟惊心。
烽火连三月，
家书抵万金。
白头搔更短，
浑欲不胜簪。

A Spring Outlook

Du Fu

The state broken, the land we keep;
In spring the town's grass grows so deep.
For hard times, at blooms I shed tears.
Parting, at birds' shrills I show fears.
Three months the beacon-fire smoke flew;
Myriad gold taels home mails rise to.
My grey head scratched to shorter hair,
Even a hairpin I can't wear.

漫　兴(其一)

杜　甫

眼见客愁愁不醒，
无赖春色到江亭。
即遣花开深造次，
便教莺语太丁宁。

Free Writing (No. 1)

Du Fu

My being drowned in sorrow is seen though;
Th' stream pavilion spring uncalled for does reach.
Unthoughtful, you've come to let flowers blow,
And bid orioles chatter too much to preach.

漫　兴(其二)

杜　甫

糁径杨花铺白毡，
点溪荷叶叠青钱。
笋根雉子无人见，
沙上凫雏傍母眠。

Free Writing (No. 2)

Du Fu

With white felt th' poplar-catkins-strewn path's laid;
With coins th' lotus-leaves-starred stream's overlaid.
The tender bamboo shoots for none to sight,
On sand by Mum, asleep th' ducklings have stayed.

漫　兴(其三)

杜　甫

熟知茅斋绝低小，
江上燕子故来频。
衔泥点污琴书内，
更接飞虫打着人。

Free Writing (No. 3)

Du Fu

Small and low the thatched cottage known to be,
Th' River swallow comes again and again.
Th' in-mouth mud drops on string and book a stain;
What's more, after flies, it bumps into me.

江畔独步寻花

杜 甫

黄四娘家花满蹊，
千朵万朵压枝低。
留连戏蝶时时舞，
自在娇莺恰恰啼。

Seeking for Flowers Alone by the River

Du Fu

Paths crammed with flowers at Huang's house around,
Thousands of flowers bend low to the ground.
Lingering butterflies flies frequently;
Free little warblers chatter happily.

赠花卿

杜 甫

锦城丝管日纷纷，
半入江风半入云。
此曲只应天上有，
人间能得几回闻。

To the Lad, Mr. Hua

Du Fu

Each day in Brocade Town string ’nd flute sounds flow;
Half to th’ River winds, half to clouds they go.
Only in the sky like tunes one can hear;
Few times they can come to the mortal ear.

绝句二首(其二)

杜 甫

江碧鸟逾白，
山青花欲燃。
今春看又过，
何日是归年。

Two Quatrains (No. 2)

Du Fu

The River green, the bird's more white;
The hills green, the blooms seem to burn.
To th' end of this spring is time's flight;
When is it for me to return?

漫成一首

杜　甫

江月去人只数尺，
风灯照夜欲三更。
沙头宿鹭联拳静，
船尾跳鱼拨剌鸣。

Free Writing

Du Fu

The river moon is a few feet away;
Th' lantern-lit night is to the break of day.
Sleeping egrets on th' sand snuggle but still,
Some jumping fish at the stern splash and trill.

春夜喜雨

杜　甫

好雨知时节，
当春乃发生。
随风潜入夜，
润物细无声。
野径云俱黑，
江船火独明。
晓看红湿处，
花重锦官城。

Good Rain on a Spring Night

Du Fu

Good rain knows the season just right,
So it will fall as spring arrives,
With wind, it steals into the night,
Quiet, it moisturizes lives.
Over the wild paths black clouds spread;
From boat lanterns alone, light looms.
Dawn sees the saturated red,
The Brocade Town's heavy with blooms.

绝　句

杜　甫

迟日江山丽，
春风花草香。
泥融飞燕子，
沙暖睡鸳鸯。

A Quatrain

Du Fu

Fine is th’ land as long daytime goes;
Sweet are blooms ’nd grass as spring wind blows.
Holding in mouth mud, swallows fly;
On warm sand, mandarin ducks lie.

绝　句

杜　甫

两个黄鹂鸣翠柳，
一行白鹭上青天。
窗含西岭千秋雪，
门泊东吴万里船。

A Quatrain

Du Fu

Amid green willows two orioles cry;
To the blue sky a file of egrets fly.
In th' window sits th' West Ridge with aeons of snow;
Out th' gate berth East Wu's ships in a long row.

望　岳

杜　甫

岱宗夫何如，
齐鲁青未了。
造化钟神秀，
阴阳割昏晓。
荡胸生层云，
决眦入归鸟。
会当凌绝顶，
一览众山小。

Watching the Mountain

Du Fu

What's lofty Mount Tai like in height?
Beyond Qi 'nd Lu, it's still in sight.
Nature's made it beauty of art;
South and North make dawn and dusk part.
Near my heart layers of clouds lie;
In my wide eyes return birds fly.
Its very top I must ascend;
To see other mountains descend.

不见

杜甫

不见李生久，
佯狂真可哀。
世人皆欲杀，
吾意独怜才。
敏捷诗千首，
飘零酒一杯。
匡山读书处，
头白好归来。

For Long I Haven't Seen Li Bai

Du Fu

For long I haven't seen Li Bai;
He feigns unrestraint, which is sad.
All rulers want to kill the guy;
Only I want to love the lad.
Bright, he has many poems to write;
Adrift, he has a cup to hold.
At Mt. Kuang your school does alight;
You should come back when you get old.

八阵图

杜　甫

功盖三分国，
名成八阵图。
江流石不转，
遗恨失吞吴。

The Eight Tactical Arrays

Du Fu

Th’ Feat shines in the Three Kingdoms Days;
Th’ name’s made through Eight Tactics Arrays.
The river flows, the stones laid true;
Th’ regret’s that he failed taking Wu.

前出塞

杜 甫

挽弓当挽强，
用箭当用长。
射人先射马，
擒贼先擒王。
杀人亦有限，
列国自有疆。
苟能制侵陵，
岂在多杀伤。

Song of the Frontier

Du Fu

Drawing a bow, you'd draw the strong;
Using arrows, you'd use the long.
To shoot a man, have his horse shot;
To catch a gang, have their head caught.
Killing ought to have its right bound;
Countries ought to have their own ground.
If aggression can be repelled,
Why should much killing be compelled?

月夜忆舍弟

杜 甫

戍鼓断人行，
边秋一雁声。
露从今夜白，
月是故乡明。
有弟皆分散，
无家问死生。
寄书长不达，
况乃未休兵。

A Recollection of My Brothers on a Moonlit Night

Du Fu

War drums make people's journey cease;
Th' fall frontier hears honks from wild geese.
Dew starting from tonight comes white;
The moon viewed at home looks more bright.
Here and there my brothers to go,
"Dead or alive" nowhere to know,
Mails take long to reach where I send,
Let alone th' war not to an end.

旅夜书怀

杜　甫

细草微风岸，
危樯独夜舟。
星垂平野阔，
月涌大江流。
名岂文章著，
官应老病休。
飘飘何所似，
天地一沙鸥。

A Thought on a Travelling Night

Du Fu

The bank grass stirs in breezy air;
A boat with a high mast berths there.
Stars hang as if broad the plain grows;
Th' moonlight floods as the river flows.
For writings a name I receive?
For health 'nd old age office I leave.
What am I like, roving around?
A lone gull between sky and ground.

客至

杜甫

舍南舍北皆春水，
但见群鸥日日来。
花径不曾缘客扫，
蓬门今始为君开。
盘飧市远无兼味，
樽酒家贫只旧醅。
肯与邻翁相对饮，
隔篱呼取尽余杯。

A Friend's Visit

Du Fu

North 'nd south of my hut spring water goes by,
Flocks of gulls but seen to come day to day.
Th' bloom-lined path never swept for any guy,
Th' wicket gate opened just for you today,
Far from town, no dainties to be the dish,
Not rich, only old wine to fill the cup.
To drink with my aged neighbor if you wish,
I'll call him to the fence to have it up.

戏为六绝句

杜 甫

王杨卢骆当时体，
轻薄为文哂未休。
尔曹身与名俱灭，
不废江河万古流。

A Playful Quatrain

Du Fu

Wang, Yang, Lu ’nd Luo start the then writing way,
On which scholars’ light remarks never end.
Your life and fame will fall into decay,
Which will not shape the rivers’ course to wend.

后游

杜甫

寺忆新游处，
桥怜再渡时。
江山如有待，
花柳更无私。
野润烟光薄，
沙暄日色迟。
客愁全为减，
舍此复何之。

A Revisit

Du Fu

The temple I once again see;
The Bridge too I fall in love with,
Rivers ’nd mountains to expect me,
Blooms ’nd willows to reveal their myth.
The thin mist nurtures the wild fields;
The evening sun brings the sand’s glow,
To which my gloom completely yields;
Where else but here ought I to go?

行军九日思长安故园

岑　参

强欲登高去，
无人送酒来。
遥怜故园菊，
应傍战场开。

Missing My Old Land of Chang'an on the March

Cen Shen

A height I so yearn to ascend,
With the wine for no one to send.
Th' chrysanthemums of my old land,
By battlefields, in bloom, should stand.

戏问花门酒家翁

岑　参

老人七十仍沽酒，
千壶百瓮花门口。
道傍榆荚仍似钱，
摘来沽酒君肯否。

Making Fun of the Old Wine Guy at Bloom Gate

Cen Shen

He still sells wine, th' seventy-year-old guy;
At Bloom Gate myriads of jars and jugs lie.
The elm seeds by the road just look like coins;
With the seeds I collected, can I buy?

月　夜

刘方平

更深月色半人家，
北斗阑干南斗斜。
今夜偏知春气暖，
虫声新透绿窗纱。

A Moonlit Night

Liu Fangping

The moon lights half the house in the deep night;
The Big Dipper slants ’nd the South Dipper leans.
One comes to feel the warmth of spring tonight;
Insects first chirp through the green window screens.

春　怨

刘方平

纱窗日落渐黄昏，
金屋无人见泪痕。
寂寞空庭春欲晚，
梨花满地不开门。

A Lament in Spring

Liu Fangping

Afterglow on the window, dusk to be,
In the room, tear stains for no one to see,
Spring comes to a close in the vacant yard,
Pear blossoms over the ground, the door barred.

枫桥夜泊

张　继

月落乌啼霜满天，
江枫渔火对愁眠。
姑苏城外寒山寺，
夜半钟声到客船。

Mooring at Night by Maple Bridge

Zhang Ji

The moon sets, crows caw and frost fills the skies;
Bank maples and boat lamps bring to sleep pain.
Out of Soochow, from Ancient Hanshan Fane,
To my very boat the midnight toll flies.

春　思

贾　至

草色青青柳色黄，
桃花历乱李花香。
东风不为吹愁去，
春日偏能惹恨长。

My Woe in Spring

Jia Zhi

Grass grows green and yellowish willows go;
Peach blossoms riot and sweet plum ones grow.
East winds cannot blow my sorrow away;
Spring days just stretches my woe a long way.

拜新月

李 端

开帘见新月，
便即下阶拜。
细语人不闻，
北风吹裙带。

Worshiping the New Moon

Li Duan

Raising th' shade, the new moon she sees,
Down the steps, she gets on her knees.
None can hear her whispers to pray;
The north wind blows her sash asway.

小儿垂钓

胡令能

蓬头稚子学垂纶，
侧坐莓苔草映身。
路人借问遥招手，
怕得鱼惊不应人。

A Child in Practice of Fishing

Hu Lingneng

A boy attempts to fish with tousled hair,
Shadow on grass, sits sideways on moss there,
Waves afar when a passer-by asks th' way,
In no answer, 'nd fears to scare fish away.

咏绣障

胡令能

日暮堂前花蕊娇，
争拈小笔上床描。
绣成安向春园里，
引得黄莺下柳条。

Ode to the Embroidering of the Screen

Hu Lingneng

At dusk in the hall way, fair th' blooms have been,
Girls vied for brushes to the frame and drew,
Stitched and placed, in the spring's yard was the screen,
Drawn down the willows the orioles flew.

题红叶

韩　氏

流水何太急，
深宫尽日闲。
殷勤谢红叶，
好去到人间。

A Poem Written on a Maple Leaf

Miss Han

Water flows, running too fast by;
We're in th' court, idling all day.
To maple leaves I say goodbye:
Fare well in the world all the way.

春山夜月

于良史

春山多胜事，
赏玩夜忘归。
掬水月在手，
弄花香满衣。
兴来无远近，
欲去惜芳菲。
南望鸣钟处，
楼台深翠微。

A Moonlit Night in Spring amid the Hills

Yu Liangshi

Hills in spring give many a sight;
I've had fun there 'nd forget it's night.
Water held, in hands the moon sets;
A bloom twirled, sweet my garment gets.
When amused, how far I don't care;
When leaving, to leave I can't bear.
I look to the south where th' bell chimes;
Deep mid the green the tower climbs.

除夜宿石头驿

戴叔伦

旅馆谁相问，
寒灯独可亲。
一年将尽夜，
万里未归人。
寥落悲前事，
支离笑此身。
愁颜与衰鬓，
明日又逢春。

Putting Up at the Stone Post Inn on Lunar New Year's Eve

Dai Shulun

Who'll come to the inn to see me?
By th' cold lamp I can only be.
On this night th' end of year draws near,
Myriad li away I stay here.
Sad about nothing I have done,
Of my lonely self I make fun.
My face sad and my earlocks grey,
The morrow's another spring day.

题稚川山水

戴叔伦

松下茅亭五月凉，
汀沙云树晚苍苍。
行人无限秋风思，
隔水青山似故乡。

Dedication to Zhichuan's Hills and Water

Dai Shulun

It's cool at the arbour neath the pine tree;
At dusk, dark the shoal and trees grow to be.
The traveller's homesickness goes unbound;
They seem my land—hills and water around.

过三闾庙

戴叔伦

沅湘流不尽，
屈子怨何深！
日暮秋风起，
萧萧枫树林。

Past the Temple of Qu Yuan

Dai Shulun

On and on the two rivers flow;
Great Qu Yuan's sadness and woe grow!
Night falling, the autumn winds rise;
Winds whistling, th' maple wood sighs.

滁州西涧

韦应物

独怜幽草涧边生，
上有黄鹂深树鸣。
春潮带雨晚来急，
野渡无人舟自横。

By a Rill West of Chuzhou

Wei Yingwu

I love only grass growing by the rill;
Overhead in the deep wood orioles trill.
In rush spring tides come, rain brought forth at night;
At th' wild port a boat berths, no one in sight.

秋夜寄邱员外

韦应物

怀君属秋夜，
散步咏凉天。
空山松子落，
幽人应未眠。

To Qiu Dan on a Night of Fall

Wei Yingwu

I miss you on this night of fall;
I walk with an ode to th' cool day.
In the bare mountains pine cones fall;
Still awake you Hermit must stay.

答李浣

韦应物

林中观易罢，
溪上对鸥闲。
楚俗饶辞客，
何人最往还。

A Reply to Li Huan

Wei Yingwu

In th' grove, I close *Book of Changes*;
Free with the gulls, I face the stream.
Chu Land many a poet ranges;
Up with whom do you often team?

塞下曲(其三)

卢　纶

月黑雁飞高，
单于夜遁逃。
欲将轻骑逐，
大雪满弓刀。

The Song of Frontier beyond the Great Wall (No. 3)

Lu Lun

While the moon was dim, wild geese soared;
At night the chief of Xiongnu fled.
To chase, th' cavalry I'd have led;
Covered with snow was the bent sword.

写 情

李 益

水纹珍簟思悠悠，
千里佳期一夕休。
从此无心爱良夜，
任他明月下西楼。

On Love

Li Yi

On th' wave-patterned mat I have my thought wend;
Th' golden time to meet falls through overnight.
From now on I'll have no mood for the night;
Let the moon above West Tower descend.

夜上受降城闻笛

李　益

回乐烽前沙似雪，
受降城外月如霜。
不知何处吹芦管，
一夜征人尽望乡。

Hearing a Tune by Flute in Surrender Accepting City

Li Yi

Before th' smoke tower, like snow is th' sand sight;
Out of the town, like frost is the moon's light.
Where the tune is played by flute I don't know;
Soldiers each look to the home land all night.

陇西行

陈 陶

誓扫匈奴不顾身，
五千貂锦丧胡尘。
可怜无定河边骨，
犹是春闺梦里人。

The Tune of West of Mt. Long

Chen Tao

Lives ignored, swearing to sweep th' Huns away;
Mid th' battle dust, five thousand troops were slain.
Pity—by th' Wuding River their bones stay;
Their young wives' men in the dream they remain.

思君恩

令狐楚

小苑莺歌歇，
长门蝶舞多。
眼看春又去，
翠辇不曾过。

A Craving for His Majesty's Favour

Linghu Chu

In the park the oriole comes none;
At th' gate butterflies swarm a ton.
Gone very soon the spring will be;
Th' grace coach has never been to me.

婕妤怨

皇甫冉

花枝出建章，
风管发昭阳。
借问承恩者，
双蛾几许长。

Complaint of a Lady, an Imperial Concubine

Huangfu Ran

Out of Jianzhang gorgeous maids go,
Out of Zhaoyang tunes by flute flow.
May I ask those with th' grace of Lord,
How long can your eyebrows be stored?

凉州词

王 翰

葡萄美酒夜光杯，
欲饮琵琶马上催。
醉卧沙场君莫笑，
古来征战几人回。

Ode to Liangzhou City

Wang Han

The good grape wine shimmers in the jade cup,
About to drink, they’re by th’ horn rushed up.
Don’t jibe at the drunk who lie on th’ war ground;
From of old, back from war, few can be found.

早梅

张谓

一树寒梅白玉条，
迥临村路傍溪桥。
不知近水花先发，
疑是经冬雪未销。

Early Wintersweet Blossoms

Zhang Wei

White jade branches of a wintersweet seem,
Far from the path, by th' bridge over a stream.
You don't know there's th' bank blossoms' early blow;
You'd suspect there remains last winter's snow.

题长安壁主人

张　谓

世人结交须黄金，
黄金不多交不深。
纵令然诺暂相许，
终是悠悠行路心。

To the Owner of This Wall in Chang'an

Zhang Wei

A friendship with worldlings needs gold;
With little gold, th' friendship won't hold.
Although one has made a promise,
His heart, like a stranger's, stays cold.

江南行

张　潮

茨菰叶烂别西湾，
莲子花开不见还。
妾梦不离江上水，
人传郎在凤凰山。

A Trip to the South of the River

Zhang Chao

Arrowhead leaves rotten, you left West Bay;
Lotuses in bloom, you are still away.
With the river my dream is always fed;
You are in the Phoenix Mountain, as said.

偈

神　秀

身是菩提树，
心如明镜台。
时时勤拂拭，
勿使惹尘埃。

Gatha

Shen Xiu

The body is a Bodhi tree;
The mind is like a mirror stand.
Wipe and whisk the most frequently;
In case dust is to be let land.

桃花溪

张 旭

隐隐飞桥隔野烟，
石矶西畔问渔船。
桃花尽日随流水，
洞在清溪何处边。

The Peach Bloom Creek

Zhang Xu

A bridge from behind the mist seems to fly;
On the west bank I ask a fishing boat.
All day as the water runs, peach blooms float;
On which side of the creek does the cave lie?

晚春

韩 愈

草树知春不久归，
百般红紫斗芳菲。
杨花榆荚无才思，
惟解漫天作雪飞。

Late Spring

Han Yu

Grass and trees know that spring will end its day,
Reds and pinks bloom, vying for spring to stay.
Willow catkins ’nd elm seeds too plain to vie,
Just knowing to twirl like snowflakes in th’ sky.

早春呈水部张十八员外

韩　愈

天街小雨润如酥，
草色遥看近却无。
最是一年春好处，
绝胜烟柳满皇都。

To an Official Mr. Zhang the Eighteenth

Han Yu

Moisturizing th' capital, light rain's found;
Seen afar, all grass, and near, none around.
It's the finest view at this time of year,
Far better than the catkin-filled scene here.

游子吟

孟　郊

慈母手中线，
游子身上衣。
临行密密缝，
意恐迟迟归。
谁言寸草心，
报得三春晖。

Song of a Parting Son

Meng Jiao

The thread the mum's hands run,
Clothes for th' parting son.
She stitches a thick way,
She fears th' late return day.
Grass, who dare have the say,
Can repay th' spring sun's ray.

登科后

孟　郊

昔日龌龊不足夸，
今朝放荡思无涯。
春风得意马蹄疾，
一日看尽长安花。

After Passing the Imperial Exam

Meng Jiao

I'm not glad to speak of th' old plight;
I am free to have my today's heart light;
My steed gallops in the spring wind;
All Chang'an's blooms one day I sight.

怨诗

孟郊

试妾与君泪，
两处滴池水。
看取芙蓉花，
今年为谁死。

A Poem of Complaint

Meng Jiao

If, your tears and my own,
To th' pool apart they've flown,
Just see the lotuses,
For whose tears dead they've grown.

劝学

孟郊

击石乃有火，
不击元无烟。
人学始知道，
不学非自然。
万事须己运，
他得非我贤。
青春须早为，
岂能长少年。

To Advise Learning

Meng Jiao

Fire will burn if you strike the stone;
Smoke will not rise if you don't hit.
Learn and you'll have wit of your own;
Learn not and you will not have it.
All things must come through your own pay;
What he gains can't stand for my strife.
When you are young, strive all the way;
How can you be a youth all life?

古别离

孟　郊

欲别牵郎衣，
郎今到何处。
不恨归来迟，
莫向临邛去。

A Poem on Parting with My Husband

Meng Jiao

I pull your robe with you to go;
Where are you leaving for today?
With you back late I won’t groan so;
A visit to Linqiong don’t pay.

寒　食

韩　翃

春城无处不飞花，
寒食东风御柳斜。
日暮汉宫传蜡烛，
轻烟散入五侯家。

On Cold Food Day

Han Hong

In spring no catkins flew nowhere in town;
On Cold Food Day east winds blew willows bent.
The palace sent candles as night came down;
Into the five lords' homes wisps of smoke went.

竹枝词(其一)

刘禹锡

杨柳青青江水平，
闻郎江上唱歌声。
东边日出西边雨，
道是无晴却有晴。

The Tune of Bamboo Twigs（No. 1）

Liu Yuxi

Willows green, calm th' River water remains;
I hear over th' River floats a man's song.
In the east the sun's out and west it rains;
Said to be gone, the sun's up all along.

竹枝词(其二)

刘禹锡

山桃红花满上头，
蜀江春水拍山流。
花红易衰似郎意，
水流无限似侬愁。

The Tune of Bamboo Twigs (No. 2)

Liu Yuxi

All over the hill wild peach blossoms stay;
Th' Shu River's spring water taps hills on th' way.
Like a man's love th' red bloom's easily gone;
Like your woe the water flows on and on.

秋风引

刘禹锡

何处秋风至？
萧萧送雁群。
朝来入庭树，
孤客最先闻。

The Prelude of the Autumn Wind

Liu Yuxi

From where was the autumn wind sent?
Rustling, it brought wild goose flocks here.
In th' morn through the court trees it went;
The lonely one was th' first to hear.

酬乐天扬州初逢席上见赠

刘禹锡

巴山楚水凄凉地，
二十三年弃置身。
怀旧空吟闻笛赋，
到乡翻似烂柯人。
沉舟侧畔千帆过，
病树前头万木春。
今日听君歌一曲，
暂凭杯酒长精神。

A Reply to Letian, Bai Juyi Whom I Meet for the First Time at a Feast in Yangzhou

Liu Yuxi

In bleak places Ba's hills and Chu's rills lie;
For twenty-three long years laid there was I.
Old times to mind, flute tunes came to the ear;
Now back home, I find everything's changed here.
Past the sunken boat a thousand ones sail;
Before th' sick tree spring ten thousand ones hail.
Today I heard the very song of thine,
To lift my spirits with a cup of wine.

浪淘沙(其一)

刘禹锡

九曲黄河万里沙，
浪淘风簸自天涯。
如今直上银河去，
同到牵牛织女家。

Waves Washing Sand (No.1)

Liu Yuxi

Winding down for ten thousand miles of sand,
Th' Yellow River rolls in winds from th' world's end.
Now I go to th' Milky Way on its ride,
Where Cowherd and Weaving Lady reside.

望洞庭

刘禹锡

湖光秋月两相和，
潭面无风镜未磨。
遥望洞庭山水翠，
白银盘里一青螺。

Watching the Dongting Mountain and River

Liu Yuxi

In peace the lake and the autumn moon stay.
Th' windless pond's a mirror in th' natural way.
Seen from far, mountain in water, jade-green,
On a silver plate a black mussel's been.

暮江吟

白居易

一道残阳铺水中，
半江瑟瑟半江红。
可怜九月初三夜，
露似真珠月似弓。

Ode to the River at Dusk

Bai Juyi

Over th' river spreads the setting sun's light;
One half of it shakes, th' other half aglow.
In the ninth moon, on the lovely third night,
The dew is like a pearl, the moon a bow.

忆江南

白居易

江南好，
风景旧曾谙。
日出江花红胜火，
春来江水绿如蓝。
能不忆江南？

A Recollection of the South

Bai Juyi

The South I so admire;
In my memory stays the scene.
Th' sun shines, th' riverside blooms redder than fire;
Spring comes, the River as good as grass green.
How can't it be my heart's desire?

问刘十九

白居易

绿蚁新醅酒，
红泥小火炉。
晚来天欲雪，
能饮一杯无？

Asking Liu the Nineteenth

Bai Juyi

I have very newly brewed wine,
I have th' brown earthen stove of mine.
As night falls it's going to snow;
Would you drink a cup with me though?

长相思

白居易

汴水流，
泗水流，
流到瓜州古渡头，
吴山点点愁。
思悠悠，
恨悠悠，
恨到归时方始休，
月明人倚楼。

Long Longing

Bai Juyi

Th' Bian water flows,
Th' Si water flows,
Down to the Guazhou old ferry they go;
To the Wu mountains goes my woe.
My thought does flow,
My grief does flow,
Until you return, the grief can just end;
I lean at the loft in rays Moon does send.

赋得古原草送别

白居易

离离原上草，
一岁一枯荣。
野火烧不尽，
春风吹又生。
远芳侵古道，
晴翠接荒城。
又送王孙去，
萋萋满别情。

Ode to the Grass on the Ancient Plain

Bai Juyi

Grass spreads lush, lush on the great plain,
With death 'nd life each year to regain.
In bush fires, to death it won't burn;
In the spring wind, life does return.
The old road wildlife does invade;
The way to the bleak town it's made;
Once again I see my friend go,
The grass heavy with parting woe.

钱塘湖春行

白居易

孤山寺北贾亭西，
水面初平云脚低。
几处早莺争暖树，
谁家新燕啄春泥。
乱花渐欲迷人眼，
浅草才能没马蹄。
最爱湖东行不足，
绿杨阴里白沙堤。

A Field Trip to Qiantang Lake in Spring

Bai Juyi

North of Gushan Fane to Arbour Jia's west;
Water just up to the bank, low clouds rest.
For sun-lit trees early orioles do vie;
Clay in mouth the swallow newcomers fly.
A riot of blooms comes to let the eye cheer;
Short grass has the horse's hoof disappear.
East of the lake I love the best to wend;
Down th' willow shades th' white sand dyke does extend.

池上

白居易

小娃撑小艇，
偷采白莲回。
不解藏踪迹，
浮萍一道开。

On the Water

Bai Juyi

A little boat a child did pole,
'Nd came back with lotuses he stole.
Trace he didn't know to remove;
To a way out duckweed did move.

花非花

白居易

花非花，
雾非雾。
夜半来，
天明去。
来如春梦几多时，
去似朝云无觅处。

Not Being Blooms

Bai Juyi

Like blooms but not;
Like haze but not.
Night sees her show;
Dawn sees her go.
Coming like spring dreams, how long can she stay?
Gone like morn clouds, found nowhere, she's away.

大林寺桃花

白居易

人间四月芳菲尽，
山寺桃花始盛开。
长恨春归无觅处，
不知转入此中来。

Peach Blossoms at Grandwood Temple

Bai Juyi

In April all flowers have met their doom;
Peach blossoms at th' mountain temple just bloom.
I oft hate to seek nowhere with spring gone,
Not knowing they've transferred here and bloom on.

后宫词

白居易

泪湿罗巾梦不成，
夜深前殿按歌声。
红颜未老恩先断，
斜倚熏笼坐到明。

A Lament for Imperial Concubines

Bai Juyi

Silk towel wet with tears, I cannot sleep;
Songs played at th' front palace on a night deep,
Grace cut off, I haven't come of old age;
Till day breaks I lean over th' incense cage.

二月二日

白居易

二月二日新雨晴，
草芽菜甲一时生。
轻衫细马春年少，
十字津头一字行。

The Second Day of the Second Moon

Bai Juyi

On the Day after a rain it clears so,
Grass and vegetables on the wild grow.
Riding steeds, some young men are in light dress;
At the cross-shaped port, they roam in a row.

悯　农（其一）

李　绅

春种一粒粟，
秋收万颗子。
四海无闲田，
农夫犹饿死。

Pity on Husbandmen (No. 1)

Li Shen

In spring a single seed is sown,
In fall ten thousand grains to own.
The world has no spare fields aground;
Husbandmen starve to death around.

悯　农(其二)

李　绅

锄禾日当午，
汗滴禾下土。
谁知盘中餐，
粒粒皆辛苦。

Pity on Husbandmen (No. 2)

Li Shen

In th' sun men weed crops at midday;
Sweat drops into the farming soil.
Who knows, grains on the plate you lay?
Each one comes from hardships and toil.

江 雪

柳宗元

千山鸟飞绝，
万径人踪灭。
孤舟蓑笠翁，
独钓寒江雪。

The River Snow

Liu Zongyuan

In all hills flying birds are none;
Along all trails found is no one.
A caped old man at the lone bow
Fishes on th' cold river in th' snow.

登　山

李　涉

终日昏昏醉梦间，
忽闻春尽强登山。
因过竹院逢僧话，
又得浮生半日闲。

Mountain Climbing

Li She

Drowsy as if drunk or in sleep all day,
Spring heard to end, to climb th' mountain I'm fain.
I talk with the monks when past th' bamboo fane;
I've idled my life's half a day away.

寻隐者不遇

贾 岛

松下问童子，
言师采药去。
只在此山中，
云深不知处。

To Seek the Recluse in Vain

Jia Dao

I ask the boy under th' pine tree;
"Master's out for herbs," replies he.
"In this mountain he is somewhere;
Deep mid th' clouds, I don't know the where."

剑　客

贾　岛

十年磨一剑，
霜刃未曾试。
今日把示君，
谁有不平事？

The Swordsman

Jia Dao

A sword stoned up for ten years though,
Shining sharp, unused yet to fight.
Today the sword to you I show;
Whoever has a wrong to right?

马　诗

李　贺

大漠沙如雪，
燕山月似钩。
何当金络脑，
快走踏清秋。

A Poem on the Horse

Li He

In the vast desert the sand is snow-white;
Over th' Yan Mountains the moon is hook-like.
When will my steed wear a bridle of gold,
To run for a battle in autumn cold?

雁门太守行

李　贺

黑云压城城欲摧，
甲光向日金鳞开。
角声满天秋色里，
塞上燕脂凝夜紫。
半卷红旗临易水，
霜重鼓寒声不起。
报君黄金台上意，
提携玉龙为君死。

The Tune of Governor to the Yan Gate

Li He

Black clouds over the town seem to drown it;
Armours in th' sun shine like golden scales split.
Horns fill the air in the autumn-hued sight;
On th' plain rouge congeals to crimson at night.
Th' red flag gets to the Yi River, half rolled.
Drums don't sound loud with frost, the night cold.
In return for the king's good done to me;
Holding Yulong Sword, for him dead I'd be.

清　明

杜　牧

清明时节雨纷纷，
路上行人欲断魂。
借问酒家何处有，
牧童遥指杏花村。

Clear and Bright—A Solar Term

Du Mu

The rain rustles on the clear and bright day;
People sad for loss travel on their way.
Where is a tavern, one asks the shepherd,
Who points to Xinghua Village far away.

泊秦淮

杜 牧

烟笼寒水月笼沙，
夜泊秦淮近酒家。
商女不知亡国恨，
隔江犹唱后庭花。

A Night's Stay at the Qinhuai River

Du Mu

Mist over the water, moonlight the sand,
Mooring near riverside inns I spend th' night.
The songstress grieves not for the loss of land,
They sing across the river *Yard Blooms White*.

江南春

杜　牧

千里莺啼绿映红，
水村山郭酒旗风。
南朝四百八十寺，
多少楼台烟雨中。

The Spring of the South of the River

Du Mu

Over miles of red and green th’ oriole trills;
Banners flutter in towns in hills ’nd by rills.
Built by th’ Southern Courts was many a fane,
Many towers age and stay in mist ’nd rain.

赠　别

杜　牧

多情却似总无情，
唯觉樽前笑不成。
蜡烛有心还惜别，
替人垂泪到天明。

Ode to Parting

Du Mu

A fond one seems but to be not stirred up,
He fails to give any smile with the cup.
The candle has a heart with bye to say,
Whose tears flow for them till the break of day.

过华清宫

杜　牧

长安回望绣成堆，
山顶千门次第开。
一骑红尘妃子笑，
无人知是荔枝来。

Past Huaqing Palace

Du Mu

Viewed from Chang’an, th’ brocade’s in piles;
Gates to th’ hilltop lift one by one.
At the steed, dust thrown up, th’ Belle smiles;
None knows lichis come on a run.

山　行

杜　牧

远上寒山石径斜，
白云生处有人家。
停车坐爱枫林晚，
霜叶红于二月花。

A Walk in the Mountain

Du Mu

A stone trail winds up th' cold hill far askew,
Where clouds arise there stand houses, a few.
I stop for a late fall maple wood view,
Than Feb blooms, frosted leaves in th' redder hue.

赤　壁

杜　牧

折戟沉沙铁未销，
自将磨洗认前朝。
东风不与周郎便，
铜雀春深锁二乔。

Red Cliff

Du Mu

The broken halberd in the sand hasn't decayed;
With a wipe, I can tell it is of the prior reign.
East winds have given Zhou Yu a helping hand in vain;
In Tongque Tower th' two Qiao sisters'd have been laid.

赠 别

杜 牧

娉娉袅袅十三余，
豆蔻梢头二月初。
春风十里扬州路，
卷上珠帘总不如。

Ode to Parting

Du Mu

Bearing grace, thirteen years old, lithe and fair,
Cardamon at th' tip in early Feb air.
On th' Yangzhou road of ten miles in th' spring breeze,
Bead curtains rolled up, no one can compare.

寄扬州韩绰判官

杜　牧

青山隐隐水迢迢，
秋尽江南草未凋。
二十四桥明月夜，
玉人何处教吹箫。

To Han Chuo, Judge of Yangzhou

Du Mu

Green hills loom and afar the water flows;
Fall ends while unwithered the south grass goes.
The Twenty-four Bridge in the moonlight bright,
You Mr. Handsome teach the flute at what site?

忆扬州

徐 凝

萧娘脸薄难胜泪，
桃叶眉尖易觉愁。
天下三分明月夜，
二分无赖是扬州。

A Recollection of Yangzhou

Xu Ning

Her parting tears Xiaoniang, shy, cannot hold;
Woe her leave-shaped eyebrows with ease have told.
With the three shares of moonlight under th' sun,
Two thirds of it Yangzhou alone has won.

夜雨寄北

李商隐

君问归期未有期，
巴山夜雨涨秋池。
何当共剪西窗烛，
却话巴山夜雨时。

A Letter to the North in the Night Rain

Li Shangyin

If you ask when I'll go home, I don't know;
With th' fall's night rain, pools in Ba's hills rise so.
When can we co-cut th' wick by the west pane,
'Nd talk with you in Ba's hills in the night rain?

乐游原

李商隐

向晚意不适，
驱车登古原。
夕阳无限好，
只是近黄昏。

The Leyou Park

Li Shangyin

It gets dark, my bad mood to send;
I drive th' cart, th' old park to ascend .
The setting sun shines and rays so,
It's just that dark's about to grow.

无　题

李商隐

相见时难别亦难，
东风无力百花残。
春蚕到死丝方尽，
蜡炬成灰泪始干。
晓镜但愁云鬓改，
夜吟应觉月光寒。
蓬山此去无多路，
青鸟殷勤为探看。

An Untitled Poem

Li Shangyin

It's hard to meet 'nd hard when departure made;
As east winds go faint, all spring blossoms fade.
Silkworms don't stop spinning silk till they die;
Candles burn away when tears will run dry.
Dawn's bronze makes her sad about th' changed hair sight;
His night chant makes her feel the cold moon's light.
To go to Penglai it's not a long way;
The blue bird would like a visit to pay.

霜 月

李商隐

初闻征雁已无蝉，
百尺楼高水接天。
青女素娥俱耐冷，
月中霜里斗婵娟。

Frost and the Moon

Li Shangyin

Cicadas gone, wild geese fly south 'nd first cry,
A high tower sees water join the sky.
With th' cold Qingnv 'nd Chang'e live low and high,
In frost and the moon to be fair they vie.

忆梅

李商隐

定定住天涯，
依依向物华。
寒梅最堪恨，
常作去年花。

Recalling the Wintersweet

Li Shangyin

From hometown I’m glued far away,
To spring blooms my thought’s drawn on th’ way.
The wintersweet the most offends,
For to bloom only last year it tends.

蜂

罗 隐

不论平地与山尖，
无限风光尽被占。
采得百花成蜜后，
为谁辛苦为谁甜。

The Bee

Luo Yin

Whether it is ground or the peak,
They take all the places they seek.
Pollen gathered, honey they make;
They toil, honey sweet, for whose sake?

金缕衣

杜秋娘

劝君莫惜金缕衣，
劝君惜取少年时。
有花堪折直须折，
莫待无花空折枝。

Clothes of Gold Thread

Du Qiuniang

Clothes of gold thread don’t you spare;
Young age of your own don’t you slay.
When the bloom is great, snap a spray;
Don’t wait to snap till sprigs go bare.

淡定从容

鸟窠禅师

来时无迹去无踪，
去与来时事一同。
何须更问浮生事，
至此浮生是梦中。

Be Poised

Monk Bird Nest

With not a trace you come and go;
How you come and you just leave so.
Don’t bother with mortal affairs,
Because man’s life is a dream flow.

节妇吟·寄东平李司空师道

张　籍

君知妾有夫，
赠妾双明珠。
感君缠绵意，
系在红罗襦。
妾家高楼连苑起，
良人执戟明光里。
知君用心如日月，
事夫誓拟同生死。
还君明珠双泪垂，
恨不相逢未嫁时。

To Master Li Sikong to the Tune of a Chaste Married Woman

Zhang Ji

I'm married, as thou early knew;
Thou have given me pearls in two.
To thee for thy love my thanks go;
To th' red silk blouse I tie them so.
My mansion connects his Majesty's Yard;
With th' halberd in th' bright light, my man's on guard.
I know thy love for me is crystal clear;
To live and die, to my vow I'd adhere.
To return thy pearls, tears and tears I shed;
Regretting not meeting ere I was wed.

秋 思

张 籍

洛阳城里见秋风，
欲作家书意万重。
复恐匆匆说不尽，
行人临发又开封。

A Thought in Fall

Zhang Ji

In th' town of Luoyang I see fall winds blow,
'Nd mean to write home a mail of thoughts to flow.
Afraid I can't tell in rush all my heart,
I ope its seal ere th' postman's to depart.

腊日宣诏幸上苑

武则天

明朝游上苑，
火速报春知。
花须连夜发，
莫待晓风吹。

The Empress' Royal Park Tour on the Eighth of the Twelfth Moon

Empress Wu Zetian

The morrow morn the park I'll sight;
Spring's coming God must be let know.
Flowers have to bloom overnight;
Do not wait till the dawn winds blow.

春望四首（其一）

薛　涛

花开不同赏，
花落不同悲。
欲问相思处，
花开花落时。

The Spring Scene (No. 1)

Xue Tao

The flowers aren’t shared when they bloom;
They aren’t shared when they meet their doom.
When I miss you if you ask me;
When they blow and fall I will be.

春望四首(其二)

薛　涛

揽草结同心，
将以遗知音。
春愁正断绝，
春鸟复哀吟。

The Spring Scene (No. 2)

Xue Tao

I twist grass into a love knot,
Leaving it to my close friend then.
Th' spring woe of mine is nearing nought;
Spring birds cry a sad cry again.

春望四首(其三)

薛 涛

风花日将老，
佳期犹渺渺。
不结同心人，
空结同心草。

The Spring Scene (No. 3)

Xue Tao

Blooms in the wind decline each day;
Th' date to meet is still far away.
If it is not true love to gain,
I've twisted the love knot in vain.

春望四首(其四)

薛 涛

那堪花满枝，
翻作两相思。
玉箸垂朝镜，
春风知不知。

The Spring Scene (No. 4)

Xue Tao

How can I bear the twigs in bloom?
Instead thoughts of you spring to mind.
Before th' mirror down my tears zoom;
Does th' spring wind know for what I've pined?

江楼感旧

赵　嘏

独上江楼思渺然，
月光如水水如天。
同来望月人何处，
风景依稀似去年。

A Thought on the Past at the Tower by the River

Zhao Gu

In thought, the tower alone I ascend,
Th' moonlight like water, water like the sky.
The one came to share the moon—where's my friend?
Vaguely like last year's is th' scene to th' eye.

送崔九

裴 迪

归山深浅去，
须尽丘壑美。
莫学武陵人，
暂游桃源里。

A Poem to Cui the Ninth

Pei Di

For a recluse's life to go,
Be sure to enjoy hills 'nd dales so,
Never learn the Wuling man's way,
At Peach Blossom Spring his short stay.

春　怨

金昌绪

打起黄莺儿，
莫教枝上啼。
啼时惊妾梦，
不得到辽西。

A Lament in Spring

Jin Changxu

I shooed the orioles away;
Not to chatter in trees were they.
The sound disturbed the dream of mine;
I was not to the place of thine.

·参考书目·

[1]（法）程抱一．中国诗歌语言研究[M]．涂卫群，译．北京：商务印书馆，2023.

[2] 蘅塘退士．唐诗三百首[M]．冷莉梅，译注．南京：江苏凤凰文艺出版社，2018.

[3] 蘅塘退士．唐诗三百首[M]．陈婉俊，补注．北京：文津出版社，2018.

[4] 蘅塘退士．唐诗三百首[M]．王宏义，注译．贵阳：孔学堂书局，2019.

[5] 蘅塘退士．唐诗三百首[M]．马宁，编注．西安：三秦出版社，2021.

[6] 胡筱颖．英语世界《唐诗三百首》英译本研究[M]．上海：上海外语教育出版社，2021.

[7] 李白．李白全集[M]．上海：上海古籍出版社，1996.

[8] 马茂元，赵昌平．唐诗三百首新编[M]．北京：商务印书馆，2020.

[9] 沈祖棻．唐人七绝诗浅释[M]．西安：陕西师范大学出版总社，2019.

[10] 中华书局编辑部．全唐诗[M]．北京：中华书局，1999.

[11] 王国维．人间词话[M]．范雅，编著．南京：江苏人民出版社，2016.

[12] 王力．王力谈诗词格律[M]．南京：江苏人民出版社，2019.

[13] 吴战垒．中国诗学［M］．上海：东方出版社，2021.
[14] 许渊冲译．唐诗三百首［M］．北京：五洲传播出版社，2012.
[15] 赵彦春译．英韵唐诗百首［M］．北京：高等教育出版社，2019.
[16] 朱光潜．诗论［M］．上海：华东师范大学出版社，2018.
[17] Paloposki, O., & K. Koskinen. A Thousand and One Translations: Revisiting Retranslation[M]// G. Hansen, K. Malmkjaer, and D. Gile (Eds.). *Claims, Changes, and Challenges in Translation Studies*. Amsterdam: Benjamins, 2004: 27-38.